OF BLOOD AND SORROW

ONE WORLD

BALLANTINE BOOKS

NEW YORK

OF BLOOD AND SORROW

A TAMARA HAYLE MYSTERY

VALERIE

WILSON

WESLEY

Published in the United States by One World Books,
an imprint of The Random House Publishing Group,
a division of Random House, Inc., New York.

ONE WORLD is a registered trademark and the
One World colophon is a trademark of Random House, Inc.

LIBRARY OF CONGRESS CATALOGING-IN-PUBLICATION DATA
Wesley, Valerie Wilson.
Of blood and sorrow : a Tamara Hayle mystery /
Valerie Wilson Wesley.
p.   cm.
ISBN 978-0-345-49271-5 (alk. paper)
1. Hayle, Tamara (Fictitious character)—Fiction. 2. Women
private investigators—New Jersey—Newark—Fiction.
3. African American women—Fiction. 4. Newark (N.J.)—
Fiction. 5. Kidnapping—Fiction. I. Title.
PS3573.E8148O34 2008
813'.54—dc22   2007029572

Printed in the United States of America on acid-free paper.

www.oneworldbooks.net

9 8 7 6 5 4 3 2 1

FIRST EDITION

Book design by Barbara M. Bachman

for Primo

"History"

The past has been a mint
Of blood and sorrow
That must not be
True of tomorrow.

—LANGSTON HUGHES

OF BLOOD AND SORROW

SMELLED HER PERFUME BEFORE I saw her. It was heady and sweet, like ripe peaches left out in the sun to rot. The lady sitting next to me at the funeral this morning had worn the same scent, and I'd wondered then what madness would drive a woman to wear something that smelled so bad. I guess if you tack a fancy enough name on a perfume, hype it big, sell it high, some poor soul will drench herself in it, even if it sends dogs howling into the night.

First came the perfume, then the tapping of heels and tinkling of bells as she sashayed her way to my office. She walked like somebody who knew where she was going, which surprised me since I'm the only tenant on the floor and didn't have any appointments.

Business had been slow, as it always is in midsummer. Luckily, I'd scored some good-paying clients in the past two months along with the usual losers who darken my door and waste my time. A hotel chain had hired me in May to catch the light-fingered thief swiping money from the till, and they were keeping me on retainer. In June, a local she's-all-that had set me on the trail of her no-good fiancé, who was doing the do with her father's ex-girl. I had two assignments lined up for the end of the month. And this afternoon, I had an appointment with Treyman Barnes II, a big-time mover in my small-time town.

For once in my life, things were sweet. I had a nice man named Larry and money in my pocket. My son, Jamal, bless his heart, was plucking my nerves with teenage angst but was doing okay despite some recent traumas. Except for this morning's funeral, the day was going fine.

I'd opened the door because my air conditioner was broken, and I'd grimly accepted the fact that a cracked window and an open door would be my only relief against the summer's heat. But an open door is an open invitation—any old thing can come crawling through.

When I first smelled the perfume, I half expected to see this morning's funeralgoer. The funeral had been for Wayne Peters, who had been Johnny's mentor when he first joined the force. The woman was Molly Holiday, an old girlfriend of my long-dead brother. She was a gentle soul with a soft, aging face that reminded me how young he had been when he killed himself. I'd be the same age myself in a couple of years, and that thought choked me up bad when I saw her. We hugged like good friends and promised we'd meet for a drink sooner rather than later. I prayed she'd change that perfume before we met again.

But it wasn't Molly Holiday who came through my door.

"Well, here we are, Miss Tamara Hayle with a *y*, you and me together again, just like them Delany sisters or somethin'. I *know* you remember me from all them years back. You spend all that money I gave you?"

If I were a smoking woman, I'd have lit a cigarette.

She had a pretty, nut brown face and a mop of fake red hair that screamed twenty-dollar hooker. Her build was slight yet muscular, and she rocked her compact body back and forth like a bantam fighter eager for a match. Except for her voice, which pops up in my nightmares, I might not have known her.

"It's Lilah Love, isn't it?" I said after a minute.

"In the flesh. You don't look as happy to see me as I am to see you. What'd you do with all that money?"

"Do you want it back?"

She threw back her head and laughed, a cackle midway between a crazy old lady's and a kid high on meth. When she was finished, she glanced back at the man in sneakers who had crept in behind her.

"This here is Turk," she said, and the man lifted his head like a dog does when his master whistles. He was taller than Lilah by a foot, and thick, like he'd spent a few years working out in the gym at Rahway prison. His thin, sallow face was marked by a long, droopy mustache that crawled down to his chin—the source of his name, I assumed. His white armless muscleman fit him snugly, the better to show off biceps that were roughly the size of my fists.

She snatched out a chair and plopped down in front of my desk.

"You can go now," she said to Turk. "I just wanted her to see you." He nodded with a smirk, then skulked down the hall, obedient hound that he was.

When he'd gone, Lilah gave me a wide, crooked grin, revealing a gold crown in the back of her mouth. "I'm just wondering how you spent all that money I gave you, that's all," she said again.

I saw where she'd spent *her* money. A nice chunk of it hung around her neck in the shape of a chain sprinkled with emerald chips meant to match the ring on her finger. Her lime green silk suit sure wasn't retail, and those Jimmy Choos were roughly the cost of a case of Moët. The one odd touch was a gold anklet adorned with tiny bells, the source of the tinkle when she walked down the hall.

When I'd met Lilah Love "all them years back," she wore a cheap red swimsuit, pink-tinted sunglasses, and an innocent grin on her teenage face. We were staying at a run-down hotel called the Montego Bay about six miles from the nearest beach in Kingston. She seemed a clueless kid trapped between a husband who beat her and a lover who didn't give a damn, and her vulnerability, along with my drunken boredom, had drawn me into her web.

I'd gotten the round-trip ticket to Kingston from Wyvetta Green, payment for keeping her baby sister Tasha out of the slammer. There wasn't much to do except drink, and the rum punches were tasting pretty good. But things got hot quick. By the end of that week, five men were dead, a dear friend lay dying, and Lilah Love, suddenly a very rich woman, had bought herself a first-class ticket to Rio.

I never figured out the role she played in those deaths. She had an explanation for everything that happened: her lover had killed her husband; the bad guys had killed her lover; all that money "just fell" into her hands. Truth belongs to the person left to tell it, and, except for me, she was the only one standing. But one of her "truths" was actually true. That was the thirty grand "plus a little extra for my troubles" she left for me in a Cayman Islands bank account.

I didn't touch that money for years, then, bit by bit, I dipped into it. The first dip was Jamal's braces. Then Wyvetta Green, who owns Jan's Beauty Biscuit downstairs, got into some trouble with the IRS and almost lost her shop. Naturally, I had to dip in to lend my girl some cash; she'd saved my butt more times than I care to remember. The dipping stopped for a while, then Jamal started spending more time on the street than he should, and I dipped in and sent him to a fancy computer camp in South Jersey. Only eighteen thousand dollars was left, and I was determined to save that for Jamal's education. It meant the difference between sending him away to school and having him live at home. The streets of my hometown were turning bad, and I wanted my son gone while the going was good.

No doubt about it, Lilah Love's money had come in handy. Yet every time I whispered the password "Montego Bay" to the banker in the Caymans, a chill went through me. I knew sooner or later the girl would show up looking for something I didn't want to give. Now here she was, "in the flesh," asking about those ill-gotten gains.

"Not talking? Well, that's your choice, Tamara Hayle. You a woman who keeps her business to herself. I liked that about you from the get. You ain't changed none." Her grin told me she had; there was no innocence left, just sharp little teeth.

"What brings you to my office this afternoon?" I pulled out my professional voice.

"Don't look like you spent too much of that money here, do it? How come you didn't get yourself a big fancy office with some of them thousands I gave you?" She added a wink, as if it were a joke between us, but she was back to the money, and that worried me.

"Because I like my office the way it is," I said, at best a half truth. Nothing has changed much over the years, and I've stopped apologizing for it. My walls remain the same dreary off-white color. The sun shining down on my intrepid orphan aloe still dims from the film on my windows. The red filing cabinet, despite the recent paint job, still looks as shoddy as homemade sin. The one recent addition is my brand-new computer with its wireless connection. I can be online in seconds, and I need to be able to do that in the business I'm in. I was as proud of it as I am of anything I've ever bought. I gave it a proud glance; Lilah's eyes followed mine.

"Well, wait a minute! Just look at this," she said. "You ain't as backward as I thought. You part of *my* generation. Did you know you can find out anything you want about anybody you want on the Net? I go online and talk to all kinds of people any time of the day or night. That's how I found out your office and address. I know where you live, too. Did you know I could do that, Miss Tamara Hayle?"

"When did you get back in town?" I said, ignoring her question.

"It was time to come back. I got some business to take care of."

"May I ask what it is?"

"I got to get back something that belong to me. Something important. Stolen property, you might say. It's mine, and I want it back."

"And what brings you to *my* office, Lilah?" I kept my voice neutral.

She studied her long, sculptured nails tipped on the ends with tiny daisies. "I need your help, Tamara Hayle."

"*Tamara* will do. We both know who I am."

"I need your help, because there's nobody else I can trust."

I stared at her in amazement. What kind of a fool did this woman take me for? A thirty thousand–dollar one, I suddenly realized.

"Besides that, you owe me," she added after a minute.

"You gave me that money no strings attached," I said.

"Don't you know by now there ain't no such thing?"

"If I had the money, I'd give it back to you, that's for damn sure."

"I ain't here about the money. That's not why I came back," she said.

"And I didn't have a damn thing to do with that shit that went down in Jamaica. Don't try to hang that anywhere near me."

"Jamaica? I ain't talking about Jamaica. I'm through with Jamaica," she said with a shrug of her narrow shoulders, but I didn't think she was.

"Then why don't you tell me what this is about."

"A lot has happened to me since I left you that day in that airport in Montego Bay. Some of it good, most of it bad. Bad thing is I don't have no more money. Good thing is, I know how to get it back. Real quick. I hooked myself up with this smart-ass boy in Rio, and he told me about all kinds of ways to get back money you lost. Rich gets richer and poor gets poorer. Did you know that, Tamara Hayle?"

"So I've heard."

"Me? I don't like being poor."

"So are you still with Mr. Rio?" I tried to move her along.

"He long gone."

I didn't ask how long or how gone.

"Second good thing is my little girl. My sweet little girl. She's gone now, too, and I want you to get her back for me."

So the kid followed the money on Lilah's list of good. "Your daughter was kidnapped?"

Her gaze shifted to a spot just above my left shoulder, always a bad sign in the telling of a tale. "You might say that, I guess, if you was inclined to put it that way. You might say that, if you was inclined. Somebody took her, that's all."

"Did you call the police?"

"You know I ain't got shit to say to the cops."

"You don't seem too upset about the kidnapping."

"I know who got her. I know why she did it. I know she won't do nothing to her, but I want my baby back. That's all. She mine, and they don't have no right to her. No matter what they think. And my lying baby sister don't got no right to nothing. What the hell do a teenager know?"

She reached into a lime green leather tote bag, pulled out a worn photograph, and gave it to me. The child in the picture was about eighteen months old, as color coordinated in pink and white as Mama was in green. She held a candy cane in her tiny hand, and her hair formed a soft halo around her plump face. Her dimpled grin made me smile.

"That's my Baby Dal," Lilah said.

"She really is adorable. I can certainly see why you call her your baby doll," I said with an appreciative chuckle.

Lilah looked puzzled. "That's her name, Baby Dal."

"Like a doll?"

"No. Like that food you get in Indian restaurants. Dal. When I was doing all that traveling in the Islands, I lived in Trinidad for a spell, and I got to liking Indian food, especially that stuff they call dal. That's my favorite food, so that's what I call her—Baby Dal."

Without comment, I gave her back the photo. "So your sister has taken your child, Baby Dal, and is holding her for ransom?"

"Something like that."

"So when and where did all this happen?" I was curious for the child's sake as much as anything else. (I've always been partial to dimples.)

"Well, I had my Baby Dal while the baby's daddy was over there fighting in that Eye-rack-ie war. Damned fool was in them special forces. Trained killer was what he was. That's what he told me anyway. Trained killer. What the hell do I need with a trained killer? I like my men tender.

"Well, I fell in love with somebody else, and when he came back, he wasn't in no shape to keep the baby or me nohow, so I left him. Then his rich daddy decided he wanted her, my Baby Dal, too, but by then Thelma Lee, my lame-ass, no-count baby sister, was keeping her for me, and she won't give her back. Claims I'm an unfit mother. Shows you what she know, don't it? She's probably going to try to get money from him herself, from my baby's daddy's daddy, who's as big a fool as his son. And I want my baby back for my own self."

"And what part do you expect me to play in this . . . situation?" *Drama* had been on the tip of my tongue, but I thought better of it.

"I want you to go over there to Jersey City and get my baby back. That's all you got to do. One short trip. I'll give you some money to give to my baby sister—that's all she probably want anyway. You can drive over there in that pretty little red car I saw you get out of this morning and bring my Baby Dal back. I'm the baby's mama, and ain't nobody gonna say I can't have her. She's mine fair and square."

As if to prove her point, she pulled out a birth certificate that stated "Baby Dal" had indeed been born to "Lilah Love Barnes" on April first. April Fools' Day. That should have told me something.

I handed the paper back.

"Me and Turk went over there to talk to her and try to give her the money, and she slammed the door right in my face."

"I thought you said you were broke?"

"Ain't that broke."

"So you went over with Turk, the guy who was just here?"

"He's my new man. Younger than me. See them muscles in his hands and arms? He knows how to use them, too. Turk told me he used to work security for a big-time gangster who done gone legit, that's what Turk told me. You know what security really do, don't you? And them arms ain't the only place Turk's got muscles, if you know what I mean, but he's about as dumb as he looks. That's one thing I learned from them old-ass guys used to follow me around with their tongues hung out: the older you get, the younger you fuck them."

I ignored that bit of wisdom and said, "So you and this Turk went to Jersey City and tried to reason with your sister, and she wouldn't take the money you offered?"

"Ain't no 'this Turk.' Just 'Turk.' "

"What makes you think I would be any more successful than you and Turk?" I asked.

She shrugged. "Bitch don't know you. You look official and shit, like maybe you a cop or something. Just go there, tell her you represent an interested party, and give her the cash."

"So she'll hand the baby over to me for a fistful of cash even though she doesn't know me from a hole in the ground?"

"Believe me. Just act like you represent somebody important, somebody big-time, and she'll do it."

I shook my head in disbelief, but that didn't discourage Lilah. "Why ain't you putting this shit down? Ain't that what private investigators do, write down what their clients tell them?"

I leaned back in my chair and took a breath. "Actually, Lilah, you're *not* my client," I said. This new song and dance had the same funky tune as the one she'd sung in Jamaica. Even the names—Thelma Lee and Turk—brought to mind Sammy Lee Love and Delaware Brown, the main players in the Jamaican fiasco. Jamaica had been a long time ago, so I didn't think she could tie me to it. But this here was some *new* Lilah mess, and I sure didn't want to get mixed up with her again.

"What you mean I'm not your client?" She narrowed her eyes.

"Well, Lilah, my schedule simply won't permit me to give your case the attention it deserves," I said with feigned regret.

"Won't take no time, I told you that. All you got to do is take the girl the money and bring back my baby. What's you doing that's so important you can't help a sister out?"

It was time for the truth, so I told it. "I'm going to tell it like it is, Lilah. There is no way in hell I'm working with you. I don't know what part you played in that shit that went down in Kingston, but I'm willing to forgive and forget. You gave me that money with no obligation. That was then, this is now. And this *is* now. I wish you luck. I truly hope you get back your child. I think we're finished here," I added with a nod toward the door.

She stared at me hard for a moment, then reached across the desk and grabbed my wrist, her long fake nails digging deep into my flesh. "*I* ain't finished yet," she said.

It was at this moment that my son chose to stroll his lanky frame through that open door.

"Hey, Ma, what's going on?" Jamal said, grinning his late uncle's good-natured grin. Lilah let go of my arm and sank back into her chair. I checked my wrist to see if she'd drawn blood. He glanced at her, then at me, then back at her. "Wow, Ma! I'm sorry, I didn't mean—"

"What the heck are you doing here?" There was no way he could miss the alarm in my voice.

"I tried to call you, but the phone must have been off the hook, and I was worried and—" He stopped midsentence, his eyes big with guilt.

"You don't have to worry about me, Son. How many times do I have to tell you that?"

"God, Ma! I'm sorry. You don't have to yell!" Those eyes were hurt and angry now.

I glanced back at Lilah, fingers now folded demurely in her lap. Slowly, she uncrossed her legs, and the soft, seductive tinkle of the anklet bells drew the attention of both me and my son.

"This can't be your little boy!" she said, rising and approaching Jamal as if she were some long-lost relative. "He's so tall and handsome, Tamara. How did you get such a tall, handsome boy? Honey, come and give your aunt Lilah a great big hug!"

In that instant, I saw my boy through this woman's eyes, and I didn't like what I saw. Jamal is well on his way to becoming a handsome man, with the good looks that have made my ex-husband, DeWayne Curtis, the incurable ladies' man he's aged into. But Jamal also has my late brother's charm and my practical sense, although this past year has made me question that particular legacy.

Confused and unsure what to do next, Jamal scanned my face for an answer, which I was too stunned to give. Finally, grinning like my brother used to do when an invitation from a pretty woman came his way, Jamal took matters into his own hands and gave his "aunt Lilah" the "great big hug" she requested. She held him far longer than appropriate and giggled coquettishly.

"Strong, too. What you doing with such a big, strong, *handsome* boy?" she said, patting his shoulders and running her fingers up his arms.

I visibly flinched, and Jamal knew he had stumbled across a dangerous boundary. Lilah broke the tension with a flick of her silverplated cell phone.

"I'm going to call Turk up here so he can meet you, honey. I hope he won't be jealous of such a strong, tall, handsome boy," she said, winking at Jamal.

"I better talk to you at home, right, Ma?" Worry topped with anxiety was in his voice.

"You got that right!"

He delivered a polite, jerky nod in Lilah's direction, avoiding my eyes altogether as he headed out the door. When he was out of earshot, I turned to confront her.

"Put that goddamn phone down before I snatch it out your hand," I said.

"What you so damned mad about?"

"If you don't know, you're a bigger fool than you look."

"What you talking about?"

"Don't even *think* about my son that way!"

"All I did was give *your* baby a hug. I'm a mama, too, so you must know how much I miss *my* Baby Dal."

"You listen, and you listen good. Stay away from me and don't come nowhere near my son. Do you understand me?"

She dropped the phone back into her bag, picked up a pen, and scribbled something on a slip of paper.

"This here is the address where my baby sister stays. She lives with my crazy aunt, Sweet Thing, and Jimson, that nasty old fool she took up with. Now *you* listen to me, and you listen good. If you want *your* baby staying safe like he is, you'd best put *my* Baby Dal back in my arms. And do it right quick—before this week ends is good."

With that she stood up and left, bells tinkling faintly as she strolled out of the room.

TWO

HAVE TO ADMIT, Lilah Love's parting crack got the better of me. Her words about my son were scary as hell, and I could still feel the sting of those nails on my wrist. Death had clung to Lilah Love like fleas to an alley cat down in Jamaica, and I didn't want her bringing those bad vibes into my life. Jamal had put on some muscle, but he'd be no match for Turk if Lilah wanted to make him pay for something she thought I owed. Did she have anything on me? I didn't think so. And if she did, what would it cost me in the end? Nothing I was prepared to pay. So I'd be damned if I let the girl blackmail me for the rest of my days. I glanced at the paper she had written her sister's address on and threw it in the trash, tossing it—and Lilah Love—out of my life.

Or so I thought.

I had less than an hour to get to my meeting with Treyman Barnes. I slipped off the fuzzy orange slippers I keep under my desk for comfort, pulled on the kick-ass heels I wear for appointments, and rushed to the ladies' room down the hall for a quick once-over. No surprises there; I looked all right, but just that. My lackluster suit fit right in at Wayne Peters's funeral but wouldn't win any prize in the allure department, which made it perfect for this meeting. I was going for a reliable, trustworthy private investigator spin. After ten years in this business, you'd think I'd have it down, but every now and then, that frightened kid who never got over her crazy mama and drink-a-day daddy takes over and self-doubt will rock me to my core.

"Don't go there, baby," I said to the mirror, lifting my chin in forced self-confidence. I wondered if Wyvetta Greene had opened the Biscuit yet. She opens late on Mondays but comes in early to do inventory. I can usually count on her for a quick boost of confidence. Truth was, meeting Treyman Barnes made me nervous as hell.

Treyman Barnes II—or "Two," as he was sometimes called—was a regular on the business pages of *The Star-Ledger* and lifestyle magazines recording the ups and downs of black folks on the rise. He was a self-proclaimed "possessor of undervalued things," a phrase usually delivered with a wink. One of those possessions was a spot in the Central Ward where kids got drunk on Saturday nights and shot each other full of holes.

"Can't control the violence of others," he'd say, eyes cast down in sorrow, when somebody brought it up. "I'm a positive man who does positive things." Positive things like that real estate firm he formed with South Jersey "interests" three years ago. Jersey City was gone, the big-time developers had devoured it, and my hometown was next in line. Blocks of my city had gone up for grabs, selling like hotcakes to the fastest wallet with the strongest connections. Barnes and his crew were gobbling up Newark like hogs around a trough.

He didn't look like a hog, though. He was plump but had a winning smile and crown of gray hair that brought to mind an aging cherub. I'd heard him called "charming" by more than one person— usually somebody looking for a handout. I'd also heard that every buck he gave, he got back in flesh.

But I was ignoring his crooked halo today, savvy businesswoman I'm striving to be. Treyman Barnes could be a valuable resource, and there have been many times when I've held my nose at the scent of a client. At least this one had money—big-time—and if I hung in there with him, his connections could pay off. I wasn't sleeping with the man, just doing business, and there was no harm in that.

Or so I told myself.

On the way out the door, I caught a glimpse of Wyvetta, orange- red hair piled high à la Marge Simpson, looking over the spare room she'd recently renovated. Inspired by Earl, her longtime, gold-toothed boyfriend, she'd set up a men's spa in her back room. A customer could get a manicure, scalp massage, and haircut all while checking out ESPN or the Playboy channel on the cable TV. She called the room a Gentlemen's Oasis and had painted the walls sea blue and black to set it off from the pink and cerise that distinguished the rest of the shop. There had only been a couple of takers, and the TV was used mostly for *All My Children* and reruns of *Law & Order*, but Wyvetta was excited by the prospect of expanding her business. I had a dinner date with Larry on Wednesday, so I decided to surprise him with a trip to the Oasis.

"Sunset Red," she answered my unasked question about her hair color when she opened the door. "I've been pouring it on so many heads, figured it was time to pour it on my own."

"Sunset?" More sunrise than sunset, the orange undertone clashed violently with her beautiful dark brown skin. "Nice," I added too quickly.

"Tamara Hayle, I can read you like a book. We've known each other too long for you to be lying to me. Now don't tell me you think something is *nice* when you don't think it is," she said irritably.

"Let's put it this way, Wyvetta: it's not one of my favorite shades." I stabbed at diplomacy. "Your natural color—"

She cut me off. "My natural color ain't shit. Well, thanks for the truth anyway. If we can't be nothing else, we got to be honest. There's too much damn lying going on in this country already than for two sistuhs to be lying to each other."

"I couldn't agree more," I said, relieved at her reaction.

She stood back and studied me critically. "And while we're being honest, when you plan to do something about them caterpillars you got crawling above your eyes? When a woman gets her brows shaped, it's an instant face-lift. Not that you need one."

I smiled and let it go. We'd been friends too long to get bent out of shape over weird hair color and fuzzy eyebrows.

"So where you going all dressed up this morning?"

"Got an appointment with Treyman Barnes."

She whistled low. "*The* Treyman Barnes?"

"*The* Treyman Barnes."

"Humph."

"Humph?"

"We go back."

"You and Treyman Barnes? How far?"

"Far enough. We went to school together," she added after a moment.

"No, Wyvetta, you're lying. You don't look old enough to have gone to school with Treyman Barnes," I said, going for forgiveness about the hair color thing.

A sucker for flattery, Wyvetta bestowed it with a grin. "Thank you, Tamara. I'm much older than I look, believe me. I know his wife, Nellie, too. One of my regulars. Big woman, very shy. I don't think she knows half of what that man does. Know-Nothing Nellie, I guess you could call her."

"So you knew him in school?" I got back to Treyman Barnes.

"Well, we weren't exactly friends. You know my parents didn't have much cash, and he was from a different social class and all, even though everybody knew about his daddy, so he couldn't hold his head all *that* high."

"Knew what about his daddy?"

"You know, what he did for a living."

"And what was that?"

She picked up a pack of hairbrushes and opened it. "Before my time."

"So what is it that Know-Nothing Nellie knows nothing about?"

She gave me a hard look, rare for Wyvetta. "Tamara Hayle, don't you let that name get out of this room! Mrs. Barnes has been a loyal customer of mine for years. And you *know* I don't talk bad about my customers."

I rolled my eyes, and we both cracked up. Wyvetta Green had been the source of so many tips about people, she deserved half my checks.

"Besides that, it's too early in the day to be gossiping about the past. And I don't know if all they say is true anyway. Go and meet the man, form your own opinion." She shooed me away, like a mother does a child, then added, "If you get your rusty butt back here before lunch, I'll do them brows for you!"

"I'll do something about my brows when you do something about that hair," I said half seriously, which made her smile. "Wow, I almost forgot why I came in. I want to buy something nice for Larry. Can you hook me up with a package?"

Wyvetta beamed at the prospect of a sale. "I got the copper, the silver, the gold, and the platinum. He sounds like a real classy gentleman. Why don't you go with the platinum? He'll get a scalp massage, manicure, pedicure, and haircut. The whole bit and two glasses of champagne."

I must have looked doubtful.

"Go on, girl. Spoil the man! You got a good one and you want to keep him. I'll give you the platinum for the gold price, how's that?"

"Okay." I handed her my credit card.

"Here, let me write out the certificate." She scribbled some words on a card, shoved it into a gold box, and topped it off with a silver bow and plastic carnation. "Just tell him to come in whenever he can. I know who he is." She handed me the box, but then the smile left her face, and she leaned toward me, delivering a warning. "You be careful around Treyman Barnes, you hear me, Tamara?" she said. Her troubled look made me uneasy.

But by the time I'd driven downtown, my worries had disappeared. There was a sense of renewal in my city. Newark wasn't Jersey City, with its high-priced condos and developers tossing around millions, but it was aiming to be better than it was. A new mayor had stepped into town along with a couple of Starbucks and Daily Soups and a collective new attitude.

Yet the city still had a ways to go. People were looking for work where there wasn't any, schools were still failing kids, and a rash of teenage shootings had ripped the spirit out of everybody in town, including me and my son. There had been seventeen deaths in the early summer, and Jamal had been touched by every single one. A month ago, Tarik, a friend since kindergarten, was walking home from a game and got shot through the head by some kid in a silver SUV. They had yet to find the killer, and that worried us both. Except for a dentist appointment, Jamal would have been walking right beside him, and I couldn't get that thought out of my head.

Violent death darkened our lives, just like it did the rebirth of the city. For all the new braces, computer lessons, and SAT classes, my son and I both knew he could be wiped out by some dead-end little bastard with nothing better to do on a Friday night than shoot somebody. I'd become so protective of my son, nagging and warning and worrying, that I was starting to get on my *own* nerves.

It's getting late, Son. Where you going, Son? Who you hanging out with, Son? Who's that kid? Who his people? Where you say he lived? Where on Bergen Street? Be careful, now. You know how things can get around here. Don't go there. Don't stay out too late. Be here when I get home from work. Stay away from that kid. Don't talk to that girl.

I'd drone on to the point where he only half heard me, and his response to all that had happened was different from mine. His devilmay-care attitude toward life and limb scared the hell out of me. Determined not to show he was afraid, he flirted with disaster—

hanging with tough kids going nowhere, coming in late, answering back in a tone that he knew would rub me the wrong way. He was still basically the same sweet-tempered kid he'd always been, but there was an edge to him now that concerned me. He studied hard and his grades were reasonably good, yet he didn't identify with the "smart kids" but rather with the boys cops look at twice when they roll down the street.

My good friend Jake was still involved in Jamal's life, but my relationship with Larry Walton, a man I'd been seeing for a year, had made things between Jake and me awkward. Our old familiarity was gone, and I wasn't sure how to bring it back.

As I drove down Broad Street, my fears about violence seemed foolish. Downtown looked like it was getting ready for business. Roads were being repaired and widened; cranes hovered above. Old stores had new awnings, and places that hadn't seen the mark of an architect's pencil in a century were being renovated, spackled, and painted.

Treyman Barnes's office was on the top floor of a prewar building, not far from where my ex-husband DeWayne Curtis had once parked his lazy behind. DeWayne had left Newark and moved to South Jersey years ago, so the clench that usually grabbed my stomach when I entered his vicinity was gone. As a matter of fact, his building didn't look like the same place. Like so many others, it was now reflecting moneyed interest—which had just moved in or had believed in the city long enough to stay put. I parked in a garage down from the new arts complex that had fired up the whole renewal thing, rode the elevator up to street level, then walked to Barnes's building.

A doorman who probably doubled as security guard sat at the

front desk doing a crossword puzzle. His pale blue uniform looked spanking new and matched the décor of the lobby, but a missing front tooth spoiled the effect, and he jerked his head nervously when he spoke.

"Hey, pretty lady, who you here to see?" he said. The building obviously had a ways to go.

"Treyman Barnes." He studied my face and pushed a soiled sign-in sheet and ballpoint pen in my direction.

"Top floor." He nodded toward the bank of elevators.

"Worked here long?" I said, making conversation as I signed the sheet.

"A while. I mostly work at nights, but the day guy got sick, and I'm filling in."

"Bet things are pretty quiet around here at night."

He leaned over and smiled. "Best job in the world being a night man in a place like this. Nobody here. Half the time, I lock things up and go into that spare room over there and sleep. Ain't a soul here to know what you're doing or where you been. Don't tell nobody, though," he added with a wink.

"Don't worry. Maybe I should sign up," I said, and we both laughed.

"Top floor, baby." He nodded again and went back to his puzzle.

Despite its new façade, the building was still old, and the ancient elevator creaked noisily to the top. The door opened to a wall of mahogany panels with a wide door in the middle distinguished by an oversized brass doorknob. Intimidated, I stood in front, wondering what to do next. Push it? Pull it? Knock? A deep male voice came out of nowhere.

"May I help you?" I glanced around the room. Security cameras were positioned in four corners.

"Tamara Hayle, here for a meeting with Mr. Barnes." The door opened electronically, and I stepped onto a gold carpet so plush I wanted to take off my shoes. The owner of the voice, a youngish man in a gray cardigan and red tie, sat at a large oak desk, empty except for a telephone and a small monitor.

"He'll be with you soon. Have a seat over there." He gestured toward a couch, which was the same color as the carpet and seemed to melt into the wall. But it was hard and uncomfortable, and made me yearn for the comfort of the carpet. I glanced around for something to read, but there was no coffee or side table. No pictures hung on the stark white walls, and no plants softened the floor-to-ceiling windows. No music piped in through invisible speakers; no workers walked to and fro with coffee or afternoon snacks. There was nothing but deadly silence, and me and this man. I sat uneasily, hands folded in lap, studying my chipped nail polish.

You be careful around Treyman Barnes, you hear me, Tamara?

Ten minutes passed, then twenty.

"Will he be much longer? I have another appointment," I said. My white lie broke the silence, and the man jumped. As if on cue, the phone rang, and he picked it up.

"Yes, sir. Right away, sir," he said with a glance in my direction. "He's ready now. You can go in."

Unless Treyman Barnes had a back stairway or had beamed up through the air ducts, it was clear to me he'd been sitting in that office wasting my good day.

"I sure waited long enough," I muttered, standing up, my legs so cramped from that horrible couch, I had to stretch them.

A button was pushed, and the door separating the two rooms pulled open. As I stepped into Treyman Barnes's office, the word *lair* came suddenly to mind.

THREE

A NARROW BLACK COUCH COILED like a snake against the pale yellow wall and curled toward a stained-glass window that threw off a bloody red glow. The carpet was gold like the one in the outer office, but the nap was short and tough like bristles on a brush. The one bright spot in the room hung on the wall—an enormous white mask sprouting yellow raffia and baring fangs that gave me the creeps. Treyman Barnes sat facing the window. He spun around Hollywood-magnate style and nodded toward a chair in front of his desk. I smiled obsequiously, swallowing my attitude about the wait. He stared at me for a moment as if getting his bearings.

"First thing, everything stays confidential, got it? Nothing leaves this office, not to nobody. For Nellie's sake more than anything else. I assume that's the way you work. It *better* be the way you work," he said.

"Confidentiality is a given," I said.

He glanced at his desk as if reading my file, then back at me. "You come highly recommended."

"Thank you."

He hesitated, as if preparing to share an unpleasant truth, then said, "My son, Troy, just got back from that war. Crazy son of a bitch. I don't know why he went over there, but he sure as hell did. Told him not to go. Told him he was making a fool of himself going when nobody else was. Half the kids he went to school with are in law school now, business school. And him? He's as stubborn as Nellie is. Went over there to fight about nothing and came back that way. My father, rest his soul, made sure I got out of Nam when they called me, and nobody even called this boy. He didn't have to go. Can't do shit for himself now. That war turned him into shit."

I and other people I knew had marched against the war, but people were still proud of the kids who were fighting and made sure everybody else was, too. I couldn't stomach a man talking bad about a boy who risked his life thinking he was doing his duty. But I kept my feelings to myself.

"And the reason you called me has something to do with your son?" I said.

"He has a baby daughter, and his ex-wife took the baby from him. I want you to get that baby and bring her to me and my wife so as we—my son, my wife, and me—can raise her. His ex-wife is a tramp."

"Does this . . . tramp have a name?"

"Lilah Love."

Oh Lord! Baby Dal born on April 1 to Lilah Love Barnes.

I took a breath and said, "Mr. Barnes, I'd like to make you aware of something. I, uh, met Ms. Love a number of years ago in Jamaica and did some work for her down there. Ms. Love stopped in my office early this morning and asked my help in finding a lost child. Her baby's name was Baby Dal. Is this the child we're discussing?"

His eyes got narrow, and his voice got loud. "Lost? What you mean lost? Kidnapped? Is that what she said? I thought *she* had her. You mean to say that dumb little bitch let somebody steal that child?"

"I only know what I was told, which is that Baby Dal is missing," I said neutrally.

"And that's another thing. Baby Dal! First thing Nellie and me are going to do is change that damn name. That's number one. Then I'll make sure that slut gets what's coming to her."

"Are you sure you're legally entitled to the child, Mr. Barnes? Despite what some might consider her . . . limitations, Ms. Love is the child's natural mother, and the law considers a mother's rights sacrosanct in matters such as this."

"Sacrosanct! Bullshit! She let the damn kid get stole, didn't she? What kind of sacrosanct is that? I don't give a shit about the law. There are ways around the law, and I know how to find them. The child is my blood; she belongs to me. As far as I'm concerned, neither one of the natural parents can raise her properly. The woman's a whore and the boy's a nut. Does she know who took her?"

I shrugged noncommittally. No sense in showing all my cards.

"How long were your son and Ms. Love involved?" Lilah had conveniently left that out.

"She trapped him into marriage with the oldest trick in the book. He was looking for something 'to believe in,' as he put it. She spotted him in his fancy uniform and knew just where he was headed. Sent him a photo of the baby and a Dear John letter a month after he got stationed in Fallujah. Probably figured the shock of it would get him killed, probably figured she'd get his insurance money."

"So why didn't he divorce her?"

He shook his head. "Didn't want to give up the baby. He was in bad shape when he came back. His mother said he needed something to keep him alive. His mother needed something, too, that would make life good for her again, and that baby was it."

"What do you mean?"

"My wife has been . . . ill for a number of years."

"I'm sorry to hear that," I said, noticing the pain in his eyes.

"I'll do whatever I have to do to make things better for her. No matter what it costs."

I nodded, understanding what he meant.

"Lilah Love came around here six weeks ago talking about how she would let my son and his mama keep the baby for a 'certain price.' Thought she was slick. Dumb bitch doesn't know who she's dealing with. I learned what to do with trash like her on my daddy's knee, and I learned that good. She comes from trash, and that's where she'll end up. In the trash. And now you say that somebody done took her little meal ticket and gone? Ain't that some shit! So I take it you're working for Lilah Love?"

"No, I turned her down," I said quickly.

"So you're available to work for me?" He didn't miss a beat.

No, sir, I'm not, said that voice inside me, the one that I should listen to but seldom do.

"Yes, sir, I am," I said without hesitation.

How could I lose? I figured. Lilah had told me where the baby was, with her "lame-ass, no-count, baby sister Thelma Lee," and had even written down where the girl was staying. Treyman Barnes was no great shakes in the character department, but I'd bet the child would be better off with her father and grandmother than her crazy mama, especially since Lilah had tried to sell her, which told me how desperate she was for cash. A desperate Lilah Love was a dangerous Lilah Love. No baby deserved to suffer through that.

Thelma Lee had the baby, and I had Thelma Lee. Had her address anyway. Baby sister was smart enough to know Lilah was *not* mothering material. All I had to do was go to said sister, tell her what was going on, report my findings back to Treyman Barnes, and broker the exchange between them—probably with cash—or ask his lawyer to do it. They'd end up fighting it out in court anyway.

"Your fee for this service?" He brought me back to the moment.

"Depends on the difficulty," I said, looking him in the eye.

He scribbled out a check and pushed it across the desk. "This should cover your immediate expenses and any lingering doubts you have about the . . . delicacy of this situation," he added with a smirk that told me he *thought* he knew me better than I wanted him to. I glanced down at the one followed by three neat zeros and had to admit he did.

"Thank you." I quickly folded the check and stuffed it into my wallet. *Out of sight, out of mind until I put it in the bank.* "I'll send you a receipt when I return to my office. It shouldn't be hard to get some leads, sir, and I'll begin my search right away." *Starting with my wastebasket.*

"I'll wait to hear from you, then." Suddenly the gentleman, he stood this time and smiled so sweetly I wondered if I was wrong about him.

"I'll call you as soon as I have any information."

As I turned to leave, a large woman and youngish man stepped into the office, and Treyman Barnes's smile faded. The man picked up the square glass ashtray that sat on the desk and hurled it hard against the opposite wall. I jumped back as shards of shiny glass sprayed across the room.

"I told you to leave me the fuck alone, you lying old bastard!" His voice shattered in the room as loudly as the glass.

"Have you lost your fucking mind coming in here and throwing shit around? But that's what happens these days, isn't it, you crazy son of a bitch!" Treyman Barnes screamed back.

The woman, who I assumed was mother and wife to these two, was a stout woman with a plain, pockmarked face and eyes with no sparkle. Her white linen suit was stylish and expensive, and I recognized her turquoise silk blouse as one I'd seen recently in a Nordstrom catalog. From head to toe, she looked the part of the rich suburban matron—diamond studs sparkling tastefully beneath short, graying hair, feet casually clad in chic tan sandals. But that secure suburban matron disappeared when she fanned a plump bejeweled hand across her mouth and stifled a cry. *Time for me to go!* I nodded at Barnes and made my way to the door.

"Ms. Hayle, I'd like you to meet my son, Troy, and Nellie, my wife," said Treyman Barnes, blocking my exit.

Troy Barnes was built like his mother but had a long, homely face that didn't fit the rest of him and that I couldn't imagine smiling. He was a sloppy dresser, and his ill-fitting suit made him look like he didn't give a damn or had gained fifty pounds quicker than he should have. I was struck by his eyes, though. They were filled with more sadness than I'd seen in a while. I wondered if Lilah Love had put it there, then realized that Lilah was incapable of inflicting soul-wrecking pain on anybody. A man might miss her in bed for a week or two, then realize he was better off without her. His sorrow was haunting; it hurt me just to look at him.

"You okay?" he asked his mother, his voice strikingly tender. She nodded, then glanced at me, embarrassed.

"You'll have to excuse my son," said Treyman Barnes, but his eyes and voice indicated I shouldn't.

"No problem." I managed a half-assed grin, eager to get the hell out of there.

"But it *is* a problem!" He glared at me, then at Troy.

"Leave Troy alone, and let the woman go, Treyman. Just let her go and find my grandbaby. Please!" Nellie's voice was firm but patient, as if speaking to a beloved but wayward child. Wyvetta had it wrong. She probably knew everything there was to know about this man, and she loved—or hated—him with everything she had in her. But she was shrewd about displaying it, crafty. She seemed vulnerable, but I sensed she always got what she wanted. I'd seen that style in other women I'd known—shrinking violets with deadly thorns.

"Nice to have met you." I edged toward the door determined to make my getaway, and I did this time. I closed the door behind me as soon as I was out, leaving them to play out whatever scene they were playing. I could hear the son screaming like a demon as I waited for the elevator.

I tried to put them out of my thoughts as I rode down to the lobby. My mind was on my money and my money on my mind, as my son says, quoting one of his favorite rappers. I'd go straight to the bank, then straight to my wastebasket, I figured. I'd had enough of Lilah Love for one lifetime, and I wanted the folks who came with her out of my world as soon as possible. But something made me glance up as I was signing out of the visitors' sheet.

I hadn't seen him in eighteen months, hadn't heard from him in ten—long enough to tell myself I didn't give a damn and that any man who waited that long to call wasn't worth waiting for. What we had— or what I'd thought we did—made no sense in daylight. Sure, there were good things about him: he loved and respected me—body and soul—in ways that thrilled me every time I thought about him. He had never lied to me and had risked his life protecting mine. I didn't know how he made his money or the lines he crossed to do it. I did know the very thought of him turned me inside out.

The sound of his voice when he said my name was an instant se-duction, and the last two hours—last twenty-four—evaporated with-out a trace. Yet I wasn't going to let my feelings about him get the better of me. I was involved with Larry Walton, a respectable, respon-sible man. We were involved in a respectable, responsible relationship, and I was determined to cool the fever that overtakes me whenever he enters my life.

"So, when did you get back in town?" I forced myself to look at him despite the danger.

Basil Dupre was an amazingly handsome man, his skin a deep cop-pery brown, nearly the color of the Blue Mountain coffee I love but can't afford. His high cheekbones betrayed his Arawak roots, his eyes, which could flash from tenderness to passion in a blink, were as mysterious and sensual as the island on which he was born. Whenever he spoke, his voice took me back to the last time we made love.

"Day before yesterday." He stood back slightly, and his eyes swept my body. "You look good, but you always do," he said with the smile that charms me.

Why, I wondered, *had I worn this ridiculous suit?*

"I called you last night. Left a message with your son. I take it you didn't get it." He was right, of course. Jamal instantly forgets phone messages that aren't for him. But how dare he assume that after ten months of silence, I would jump to the phone the moment he called?

"What are you doing tonight?" He didn't wait for my answer.

"Busy." It was a half lie. Larry had mentioned he might drop by, but it wasn't definite.

"Tomorrow night?"

"Sorry."

"When?"

"Never."

"So, I've waited too long?" His smile teased me, as if we were playing a game, which was what our conversations always became—a playful seduction that usually ended in bed.

But I wasn't playing this time.

"I'm seeing someone now. I've been with him for . . . well . . . let me see . . . ten months." I said it with a schoolmarm's scolding tone and raised eyebrow so he'd get the connection.

"Ten months?" He got it.

"What did you expect?"

His sigh was sorrowful but unconvincing. "You know my life,

Tamara. You know how things go with me. You know me as no other woman does."

"Oh, shut up!"

"It's the truth. Don't deny it."

I avoided his eyes because I knew it was. Yet some connections are meant to be broken.

"I never stay too long in one place. Except home, of course. If you needed me, you should have called me. You know how to reach me, and that I'm here for you. Always."

"But I didn't need you," I said offhandedly with a dismissive head toss; it had the desired effect. Disappointment, then a weary sadness, shadowed his eyes. I'd never seen *that* before.

"I'll be in town for a while. I want to see you. Will you call me? Please."

Begging after all these years?

"Take care of yourself, Basil," I said, and walked away with every bit of will I could muster.

FOUR

ASIL WAS ON MY MIND when I got home that night, but Jamal wasn't far behind. I was still angry at him for showing up like he had in my office. I never know what kind of nut will stroll in from nowhere, and Lilah Love was just the kind of nut I didn't want him to meet.

I was also ticked off about him forgetting to mention Basil's call. I certainly wouldn't have called the man back, but it sure would have put a bounce in my step to know he phoned. So the minute I walked through the door, I yelled for Jamal to come downstairs.

"Down in a minute, Mom. Got to log off." He was in his room on that computer—again. Truth was, I really didn't want to know what he found so interesting. I'd put restrictions on various sites, but when it came to the Internet, Jamal could outthink me at every turn. If he wanted to access a site or chat room, there wasn't a heck of a lot I could do. My computer skills were limited to e-mail and basic re-search, and he knew it. I was sure he and his friends had visited the various "restricted" sites that teenage boys visit, and hopefully they were no worse than the porn magazines of my day. There were no expenditures on my credit cards, so he hadn't gone down *that* path. All I could do was trust the good sense of the boy I'd raised, and for the most part I did. I suspected he was better off sitting behind that desk than roaming the streets with some wannabe thug.

"Not five minutes. Now!" I sorted through the usual pile of bills, cheap catalogs, and junk mail, smiling to myself as he bounced downstairs. It seemed only yesterday that he could barely make the first step. His long legs took them two at a time these days, three if he was in a hurry.

"Slow down, Son, before you break your neck!" I clucked my usual warning as he bent down and bestowed his usual peck of a kiss on my forehead. That was another thing—how far down he had to bend.

"What's for dinner?" He headed to the refrigerator, opened it, and gazed dreamily inside as if he were watching a movie. I playfully shoved him aside and pulled out a covered bowl of leftover beef stew I'd made in the Crock-Pot the day before.

"Yuck!" he said. "It's too hot for stew. That's winter food."

"Would you rather have it cold?"

"Come on, Mom!"

"Maybe you should try cooking once in a while," I said, remembering the old days when he was younger and would heat up a can of soup or baked beans if he knew I was running late.

"If I'd known we were having *that,* I would have," he shot back with a good-natured grin.

"As much as you ate last night, we're lucky we have any left," I cracked, glad to be joking with him again. I added some water to the stew, poured it into a pot, and turned it on low.

Easy banter with Jamal was hard to come by these days. He was often sensitive to criticism and critical of me. Adolescence had brought on some of this attitude, but the death of his friend had deepened it. My friendship with Larry had also taken its toll. It was hard to gauge how Jamal actually felt about this new man in my life. Some days he seemed to cheerfully accept and enjoy his company, other times the mere mention of Larry's name rubbed him the wrong way. I suspected Jamal still had hopes that me and Jake Richards would get together someday. He's known Jake all his life, and I've known him longer than that. Through the years, I'd explained more than once that Jake and I were simply good friends and would remain that way, but I hadn't convinced Jamal, and hope sprang eternal. (Maybe because I hadn't entirely convinced myself.) Nevertheless, Larry was here to stay, so there was even less chance for me and Jake, despite my son's fantasies.

For his part, Larry wasn't particularly sensitive to Jamal's feelings. On more than one occasion, he'd suggested that it would "do the boy some good" to spend more time with his father, which suggested that I hadn't done the boy as much good as he needed. I knew Jamal had overheard him at least once and been hurt by his veiled criticism, but I didn't bring it up to either of them. For so many years, it had just been me and Jamal, and it felt good to finally have a steady man in my life. I was damned tired of being alone, and I didn't want to wreck it. Yet as Larry and I grew more comfortable with each other, I missed the easy talk that Jamal and I had always shared, and I caught myself wondering every now and then if Larry was really what I needed.

The phone rang as Jamal was setting the table. He dashed to get it, then handed it to me without comment; his attitude told me it was Larry.

"So, sweetheart, how did your day go?" The sound of his rich, sexy baritone made me grin. I shared my day in general terms, focusing on the good, skipping the bad. Larry had hinted more than once that if we were going to make our connection permanent, I should consider finding a new profession. His tone suggested that he didn't consider "private investigator" a fitting vocation for his wife, which annoyed the hell out of me, but I kept it to myself. Oddly enough, that was one thing he and Jamal had in common—both of them felt I should make a living doing something else.

"What? No gun battles, crazy people, loser clients?" he said with a forced chuckle I wasn't in the mood to hear.

"No. None of the above happened. It was a good day. A great day!" I told the lie with strained patience. "Larry, we've been through this before. This is what I do. I'm a PI; you're a used-car salesman."

"I prefer the term *preowned*. But you have to admit, the criminal element in your world doesn't enter mine," he teased.

No, they just run it, I thought, but said with forced cheer, "Are you gonna drop by tonight?"

"No, not tonight."

"But we're still on for Wednesday, right?"

"That's why I'm calling, sweetheart. Afraid not. Wednesday is election night at the club, and I've got to be there. I think I mentioned I'm running for vice president."

Ah, the club! "Yes, you did."

When we first met, he'd resigned in protest. The "club" was a rich businessmen's association in Newark that had no female members and had *literally* shown me the sidewalk when I'd snuck into a private lecture. At the time, Larry made a big deal out of resigning, but he'd recently rejoined, claiming it was easier to transform institutions from the inside. His decision to run for office was one way to help things along, he claimed. I only half believed him.

"I'll make it up to you on Thursday, I promise."

"I'm going to make you keep that promise," I said, forcing a smile into my voice. "I got you something special. I think you'll really like it."

"Surprise? All I need is you, baby. All I need is you. See you Thursday night." He hung up before I could say anything else. My disappointment must have been written on my face.

"Stood you up, huh?" Jamal said with a smirk.

Ordinarily, I wouldn't have reacted to such a sassy, poorly timed remark. I might have made a joke of it, shook my head, rolled my eyes, or simply ignored him. Unfortunately, this was *not* one of those times.

"Mind your own damn business," I said with fire in my eyes.

"You're always minding mine," he shot back.

"Who the hell do you think you're talking to?" I stood up to confront him, only to have him look down at me.

"Who else is in the room?"

"Boy, you better watch that damn mouth!"

"Well, then, please don't curse at me, Mom. You've cursed at me three times, and I don't like it!"

"When I curse at you, boy, you'll know it," I said. We stared at each other for a tense, hot minute.

"It's not my fault you had a bad day." Jamal backed down in a small voice.

"Who said I had a bad day?"

"I'm out of here," he said with an exaggerated shrug even though he was standing right in front of me.

"You're not out of anywhere until I'm good and ready to let you go! You stay where you are! I have something else to talk to you about," I said, my voice raising by two octaves.

Parenting columns advise never to confront a teenager about his behavior when both of you are angry. Better to let things cool. Take a deep breath. Don't let words roll out your mouth you can't pull back. I forgot all those parenting columns in a heartbeat—and my heart was beating fast.

"You listen to me, boy, and you listen good," I said, mad at everyone, and everybody's mama, who had done me wrong that day. "I *never* want to hear your mouth about my relationship with Larry Walton or any other man I'm seeing, do you understand me? I'm a full-grown woman, and I sure don't need to hear any mess from a half-grown man!"

"But, Mom, I'm—"

"And another thing." I was on a roll. "You know very well you're not supposed to come to my office without calling me first. What in the heck did you think you were doing, strolling in there this afternoon, talking to that crazy—"

"Well, she seemed nice enough. I—"

"You don't know nice from a hole in the wall, and just when did you stop giving me messages? When somebody calls me on the phone, I don't care who it is, you make sure you tell me they called, you got that?"

"Well, I forgot—"

"And while I'm at it, I'm sick to death of your attitude. Clean it up!" I said, finishing it off with a dramatic head roll.

It was Jamal's turn now. "I guess I can't do anything right, can I? Maybe your big, bad boyfriend has a point."

I stopped dead in my tracks. "What do you mean?"

"About me living with my dad, that's what I mean. If I can't do anything right, maybe I should get the hell out of here. Maybe I should go live with him for a while. He wants me to, I know that!"

"I didn't say I didn't want you, I just said—"

"My dad wouldn't get mad if I visited him at his office. My dad—"

"So you want to live with DeWayne?"

"What's wrong with that?"

"So you want to live with DeWayne?"

Jamal looked at me and then at the floor.

"Well, if you want to live with your jackass of a father, then go right ahead and do it!" I said, turning my back on him.

"Don't call my dad a jackass! He's not a jackass!" He turned and bounded up the stairs as quickly as he'd bounced down.

"I'll call him whatever I want to, and as far as I'm concerned, that's exactly what he is!" I screamed back.

The stew on the stove chose that moment to burn.

"Damn it to hell!" I screamed, grabbing it off the burner and tossing the whole mess into the garbage, nearly burning my hand in the process. The smell of burned stew turned my stomach. Jamal was right. Beef stew was a disgusting choice for a summer meal. What kind of mother was I? Appetite gone, I uncorked a bottle of merlot, poured myself a cork-filled glass, and slumped down on the living room couch.

Why in God's name had I yelled at the boy like that? I asked myself as I finished off one glass and quickly poured another. He was a kid, and as kids go, I had it good; I knew that. I'd always made a point of never bad-mouthing DeWayne Curtis in front of him, although he sure deserved it. DeWayne was part of my son, and to put him down was to put down part of Jamal, and I never wanted to do that. Usually, I had control of my temper. I'd go into the bathroom and call him every filthy name I could think of, but Jamal never heard me. Why had I done it tonight? What was all that about?

It was about a broken air conditioner I'd bought with good money and remembering my brother at that funeral and Lilah Love with her brazen, silly self and Treyman Barnes and his crazy-ass son. And it was about Larry and what he didn't do for me, and Basil and what he did.

"Fuck!" I screamed aloud, swearing yet again in that curse-ridden room. I had crossed the line with Jamal, hurt the one person in my life that made everything worthwhile. I poured what was left of the wine into the sink and went to the bottom of the stairs.

"Hey, Jamal, I'm sick of stew, too. You feel like Red Lobster tonight?" I called up, summoning the one name that always got a positive response.

No answer.

"Hey, Jamal! Did you hear me?"

Truth was, I didn't feel much like Red Lobster either.

I opened a can of tuna fish, added too much mayonnaise and relish, and spooned the mess on top of some Ritz crackers. Too lazy to change my clothes, I tucked a paper towel into my blouse for a bib but spilled soupy tuna down the front of my suit anyway. What a slob!

I watched a sitcom on TV, then settled into my favorite cop show. After the news, I checked my office phone, half hoping that Basil, inspired by the sight of me, would try again. No such luck. Instead, a weary little voice that sounded like a kid's came across the line in one long, scared breath:

"Miss Hayle, this is Thelma Lee Sweets, Lilah Love's baby sister, but I call myself Trinity 'cause *Thelma Lee* sounds country, and I know Lilah's doing business with you 'cause I just know, but whoever wants this baby back can have her 'cause I'm sick and tired of all this drama around this child, and it's getting scary with people following me around and shit, and if you come over here first thing tomorrow morning, you can have this Baby Dal back."

She took a breath, as if those words took everything out of her, then gave me her cell phone number and the address in Jersey City I'd fished out of the trash before I came home. I called her back, leaving a message on the voice mail that answered, saying I'd see her in the morning.

I played the call back again, listening for any missed nuance. Not for the first time and probably not the last, I regretted letting go of Karen, the trusty operator from my former answering service. I could always count on her for a laugh or an off-the-wall crack on people who called me. I wondered what she'd say about Thelma Lee Sweets aka Trinity.

I called the number I had for Treyman Barnes and left a message telling him that matters had resolved themselves quicker than anticipated, and I'd located the woman who had his grandchild and she had agreed to give her up. I gave him Thelma Lee's address and number and suggested that he and his wife meet me nearby so that I could give the child to them after I picked her up. I ended with a cheery promise that by this time tomorrow, they'd be kissing their grandchild good night.

I should know by now that when things stir that easy, there's always something lumpy at the bottom of the pot. Yet there I sat, sated by wine gulped too fast and greasy tuna fish, congratulating myself on earning a week's wages without a day's hard work. I went upstairs feeling good, not even bothered by Jamal ignoring my knock at his door.

"Stay mad, I love you anyway," I called out, amused by his stubbornness. Sick of the world and slightly drunk, I filled my bathtub with lavender bubbles and soaked until my toes got wrinkled; then I went to bed remembering the last time I made love to Basil Dupre.

FIVE

WOKE WITH A START, heart beating fast. I was lying on the same old bed, staring at the same cracked ceiling that stretched across the same room I'd slept in for more years than I care to remember. But my stomach was clenched so tight I couldn't catch my breath.

Just getting old.

That was what my grandma would say when she woke, one hand clutching her heart, the other holding me. I'd creep into her room when my parents fought, seeking peace in the softness of her narrow bed. When I think of her, I can still smell the camphor sweetened by lavender cologne that lingered on her sheets.

Just getting old, that's all, baby. What you don't think about in the day meets you when the sun go down.

Are you scared, Grandma?

Getting old passes, too.

"Ain't that old, Grandma!" I said aloud to the memory of her and those times. *Ain't that old.*

Yet there was that tightening beneath my heart.

Jamal!

Always my first thought when I need to worry. I glanced at the clock: 8:45. I'd overslept, and Jamal was in summer school going for those extra credits, if he knew what was good for him. I yawned and stretched, still tired as hell; Lilah and Barnes had really put me through it.

"Jamal, you better be up and out!" I yelled just in case.

No answer. Good. At least he'd started *his* day. I felt bad about the fight we'd had last night. I'd make it up to him tonight. Red Lobster with all the trimmings would be a start. His taste in seafood grew more expensive each year; popcorn shrimp was a thing of the past, but Barnes's check would clear in a day or two, so I could afford to play big spender.

I grinned when I thought about that check. I had a lot to be thankful for this morning. I said a silent prayer of gratitude for everything that came to mind, then jumped into the shower and got dressed. I gulped down a cup of coffee while spreading butter on an English muffin I'd eat on the road, then headed to Jersey City.

The sun was shining brightly as I entered the old port city, second only in size and people to Newark. Chilltown, as folks here liked to call it, was flying high these days, flaunting the style and money my dear hometown could only aspire to. Eleven miles of waterfront on the Hudson had made it a developer's dream, and the city was strutting its wealth.

It hadn't always been that way. The violence and blight that swept through Newark in the sixties and eighties and was still having its way had run through Jersey City, too. There was a time when the roughest dudes in the Central Ward avoided the place like the plague. Then the city came into its own. Rich folks not quite rich enough for Manhattan suddenly discovered that "interesting" little spot across the river closer to Wall Street than Fort Greene or Park Slope, and before you knew it, things had turned around. The "gentry" moved in and gentrified the deserted Victorians and decrepit factories, and suddenly they were selling for close to a million. The city still had pockets of poverty as deep as those in Camden and Newark, but nobody talked about them much, and folks tended to forget they were there. It wasn't like Newark, with its spate of teenage killings that had brought down property values and haunted my son. Our new mayor, kid that he was, was getting good press. For the sake of my son, I prayed he deserved it.

Ken Gibson, Newark's first black mayor, was running things when I was a girl. On the day he won, my daddy and all the brothers on our block toasted the man with anything they could get their hands on—Johnny Walker Red, in my father's case—which laid him out for damn near two days. The riots in '67 brought Gibson in but changed my town forever—the riots and the highway that ran through the middle of the well-kept homes of Newark's middle class. A highway through the center of town will scar a city's soul as fast as a crime wave, and we had both.

This tale of two cities was running through my mind as I looked for Thelma Lee Sweets's address. I was late, and I knew it. The girl had said morning, and it was going on eleven. I was surprised I hadn't heard from Barnes. He'd been so eager to get his hands on the child, it was strange he hadn't called. I wondered if he'd decided to come and get his grandchild himself.

If you come over here first thing tomorrow morning, you can have this Baby Dal back.

Scared little Thelma Lee was as serious about getting rid of the kid as Barnes was about getting her, and it would be better for everybody involved—especially me—if she gave the child directly to her grandfather. I sure didn't want Lilah Love hauling me in on a kidnapping charge for being the go-between. I halfway hoped it would go down like that. Then I could go back home, grab a second cup of coffee, and start my day doing what I like to do best—absolutely nothing.

I thought again about Basil Dupre, always there when I wanted to forget him. What the hell was he doing in Barnes's building anyway? Was he up to no good with Barnes, or was this just some cosmic coincidence come to kick my ass once again? I'd have to ask him the next time— I stopped myself right there. There would be no next time. And yet . . . There was always "and yet" with Basil Dupre.

The skyscrapers of Manhattan sparkled in the distance as I drove onto Ogden Avenue and pulled in front of a ramshackle gray Victorian. The three-story house was a tacky rebuff to its neighbors, which peered down like queens at a puddle of pee. But I knew enough about real estate to see that this one had been royalty once, too. The steep gabled roof was trimmed with so much gingerbread, I could almost smell it, and the wraparound porch with its ornate carvings demanded elegant women in flowing white gowns and pale blue ribbons. With its view of Manhattan and well-to-do neighbors, this one was a jewel; it just needed a rich somebody to discover and polish it.

But the place had a sad-sack look to it now. The roof needed shingles yesterday, and weeds had taken root in the gutters. Some optimistic soul had planted pink impatiens on the edge of the sun-scorched lawn, but that was it in the landscaping department. I got mad at Lilah all over again. The girl could deck herself out in Jimmy Choos but couldn't send a dime to folks who clearly needed every penny. But if she grew up here, surrounded by wealth on either side, I could understand her material-girl obsession. I realized again that I really didn't know squat about Lilah Love except what she'd told me, and that usually wasn't worth a cup of spit. I assumed, though, that most of what she had told me about the baby was true.

I stepped on the porch and rang the doorbell, and somebody darted behind the sheer, drawn curtain. I knocked for good measure.

"Who there?"

It was an old woman's scared, cautious voice, not the high-pitched, fast-talking one I'd heard last night.

"Good morning, ma'am. My name is Tamara Hayle. I'm a private investigator. I have a meeting scheduled with Thelma Lee." I stepped close to the door and listened. No sound of a baby.

"Private investigator? Jimson said you called. What you want with my niece?" Although I'd left the message for Thelma Lee, she must have heard about it. I wondered if she'd bothered telling her.

"I'd like to come in and talk to Thelma Lee if I may. I'm going to give you one of my business cards. You'll find the telephone number of the public defender's office on the back. Please give his office a call, and he'll verify my identity." I scribbled Jake's number on the back of a card and shoved it under the door. Jake's name followed by *Esq.* was always good for a pass. I heard what sounded like dead bolts turning, and she cracked the door, peered at me across the chain, then stood back so I could enter.

I stepped into an old-fashioned parlor with spacious high ceilings and long, narrow windows that dropped to the floor. The corner fireplace boasted its original mantel, although the marble was stained and darkened with dust. Stacks of old newspapers and dank, dusty curtains gave the room an unpleasant musty smell, but sunlight drifting in from the windows caught the intricate scrolls carved on the molding. The cheap braided rug couldn't conceal the dark pine floors that it covered. This place was, as they say, the *real* thing.

An ancient TV blasted from a makeshift coffee table, and the green sofa behind it looked as if it had been dropped in from a 1960s sitcom. Two matching black cups were next to the TV, and a baby's high chair with a soiled pink bib tossed on it leaned against a back wall. The smell of burned toast and fried bacon drifted in from what I assumed was the kitchen.

The woman herself was stocky and moved awkwardly, but her face was pretty, with flawless red-brown skin and high, angular cheekbones. Bright strands of silver ran through her silky black hair, which she wore high on her head in an unruly bun reminiscent of Mrs. Butterworth. But she had probably been as much a beauty in her day as this old house was; time and hard luck had worn them both down. I put her in her early seventies, but she moved like someone older. Her red chenille housecoat was buttoned to the top and looked as threadbare as the couch to which she led me. Avoiding my eyes, she pulled a Marlboro out of a purple case and lit it, pulling the smoke in hard and blowing it out harder.

"Beautiful place you have here." I made a stab at conversation, and she smiled.

"It's all I got, this house; love it like kin. Each and every soul I have ever loved been part of it." I was as struck by her candor as I was by the sorrow in her brown eyes.

"Did Thelma Lee tell you she'd asked me to come?"

She shook her head, and her eyes were blank. "She didn't tell me nothing."

"Does she live here?"

"Yes, she does."

"And the baby?"

"She stay here, too."

I wondered how much she knew and what I should tell her. Best to start with the truth—or a piece of it.

"I'm working for the baby's grandparents, Mr. and Mrs. Treyman Barnes. They hired me to find their grandchild, who is missing. I received a call from Thelma Lee last night, and she told me that she had the child and was eager to turn her over to the Barneses. I'm here to pick her up."

"She's just the cutest thing I've ever seen, that baby, ain't she? Just like her pretty little mama."

"Yes, she is. Is Thelma Lee here?" Best to get this over and get out as soon as I could.

"You see her sitting here? I don't see her sitting here. Unless she turned invisible, she ain't here. You think she invisible?" She said it with a cackle that surprised me; the woman definitely had an edge. I remembered then that Lilah Love had called her Sweet Thing. Maybe folks called her "sweet thing" like they'll call a six-foot kid "little man," chuckling whenever they said it.

"Do you know where she is?"

"Heard the phone ring this morning, then I heard her hightail it out of here before you knocked at the door." She picked up the cup and took a sip of whatever was in it.

"Did she say who it was?"

"Nope."

Probably Barnes, I thought. "Before we go any further, let me get your name." When I did my report for Barnes describing our conversation, "Sweet Thing" wasn't going to get it.

A door opened suddenly, and the smell of breakfast food filled the air. "Call her Miss Edna; that's her given name. Miss Edna Sweets. I call her Sweet Thing, but that just for family," said the man who walked through it, holding a slice of bacon in one hand and coffee in the other.

"You here about Thelma Lee and that damned baby, ain't you? You here about that call. You watch too much of this thing, honey," he said to Sweet Thing as he walked over to the television and switched it off. "The Man feed you all kinds of shit on this goddamn thing. You can't trust nothing he got to say. Don't you know that by now?"

"How did you know about that? About Thelma Lee?" Sweet Thing asked, as perplexed as I was.

"I know everything that affects you, baby. Everything," he said with a tender smile, and kissed her on top of the head. He was roughly the same age as Sweet Thing but built like a boxer, with broad, thick shoulders and a muscular chest. He walked like a young man, too, a strong one, with a bouncing swagger and no hint of a stumble. He had the look of a Masai warrior—sharp cheekbones, pretty lips that curled slightly, a scar on his cheek as angular as a tribal mark. I could feel the hard calluses on his palm when he grabbed mine and shook it. A workingman's hand, like my father's had been.

"Jimson. Jimson Weed. That's what they used to call me, the same way I call her Sweet Thing, 'cept she never called me that 'fo' I told her to."

"Nice to meet you, Jimson." I couldn't bring myself to say Mr. Weed.

"Jimson Weed Carter, to be exact." He winked naughtily, as if it were a dirty joke. "You don't know what jimsonweed is, do you, girl?"

"I'm afraid you've got me there."

"That's what some folks used to call marijuana back in the day. I used to smoke so much of it, weed that is, when I got out of the service back in '67, the name stuck, like a lot of other stuff that never leaves you. But they all dead now. All of them." He pulled a folding chair in from the dining room and sat down next to us. *Too close*, I thought.

"Funny how things come back, ain't it? They called it pot in the fifties, smoke in the sixties, grass in the seventies, now it's back to weed. Shit don't never go nowhere. Just back to where it come from when you don't expect to see it."

I smiled agreeably like I knew what he was talking about.

"You want some breakfast?"

"No, thank you."

"I work late. Night shift. Just got home. I'm eating breakfast when most people be eating lunch. What you want to know about that baby?" As he finished up his bacon and gulped his coffee, I told him what I'd told her. He leaned toward me, listening intently.

"I don't want nobody making trouble for Sweet Thing, you hear me?"

"And not for Thelma Lee, either. Not for Thelma Lee," Sweet Thing added.

"I didn't come to make trouble for anyone, but Thelma Lee is not the baby's mother, and she has no custodial rights," I said, shifting my attention away from Jimson Weed and back to Sweet Thing.

"That damn Lily ain't fit to be nobody's mama," said Jimson Weed.

"Don't you talk about my Lily like that, Jimson. It ain't her fault what happened! Don't you ever, ever talk about my Lily like that!" Sweet Thing spoke softly, but anger bubbled underneath the sweetness.

"I ain't talking about your Lily," he said, suddenly meek. "That is over and done with."

Lily, I assumed, was Lilah Love. Changing your name appeared to be a family trait. I recalled what Lilah had said about them: my crazy aunt, that nasty old fool, my no-count baby sister. Except for Sweet Thing's half-assed defense of Lilah, there seemed to be no love lost between any of them.

I thought about my own family then, my quick-to-strike mama and drunk of a daddy, my shot-himself-through-the-head brother, and Pet, running for cover from the whole damn lot of us. What would my dead people say about me?

"I'm not representing Lilah Love but the grandparents of the baby," I said, quickly coming back to the here and now.

"She talking about Treyman Barnes," Sweet Thing whispered.

"I know who she talking about."

"I don't want to tangle with Treyman Barnes, Jim," Sweet Thing said, her voice trembling.

"Don't worry, baby, I won't let that happen. Never!" Jimson took her hand in his, and I was touched by the tenderness in his voice and in that gesture.

"Was Treyman Barnes the person who called her this morning?" I asked.

"Ain't nobody talking to you!" he said, the anger in his voice surprising me.

"I'm talking to you," I said, getting tough. "Is he the man who called to speak to Thelma Lee this morning?"

"You think Treyman Barnes deserve that baby?" he asked. "I know what Treyman Barnes is. You think he deserve that baby?"

"I have no idea, and it's not my decision anyway," I said, striving to sound reasonable. "I just work for the man."

"Then you working for the Devil!" Jimson Weed said evenly, his eyes not leaving mine.

For a moment, his voice, with its streak of old-time religion, brought back my grandma, but hers was always softened by compassion and love. Surprisingly, though, I was hit by a stab of shame like the kind I used to feel when I was a kid.

Never be about the Devil's work, my darlin'. Never be about that.

I shoved that memory back where it belonged.

"It's not my place to judge, Mr. Carter," I said. Truth was, I'd probably worked for "the Devil" before, usually unaware of his horns and tail until he singed my hair. But this particular devil—if that was what he be—had paid me well for my burned scalp, and I had a growing son to feed.

"Are you trying to tell me that Thelma Lee isn't here because she met with Treyman Barnes this morning?" I pointedly asked Sweet Thing.

"She ain't trying to tell you shit!" said Jimson Weed.

"Then where is Thelma Lee with Lilah Love's baby?" I turned to him now. "I don't want to get the police involved, but stealing a child is kidnapping. I represent the child's rightful family, who intend to fight for custody because they believe that Lilah Love is an unfit mother, as you said yourself a few moments ago.

"I was told last night that Thelma Lee would be surrendering the child to me this morning so she can be returned to her grandparents. I'm here to make sure she keeps her word."

"But we're rightful family, too!" said Sweet Thing. "That baby is part Lily, so we have a right. Just 'cause they have money don't give them the right to claim her."

"I think that may be up to the courts to decide," I said, wishing like hell I hadn't been put in this situation. Lilah Love had managed to get me again.

"But Thelma Lee is just a child her own self! She don't know what she's doing!" Sweet Thing buried her face in her hands. "We don't want to get that girl in trouble. She's just trying to do right by the baby. Trying to keep her away from evil."

"But evil is always in the eye of the beholder," I said.

"If you don't know what evil is, then you evil, too. I know deep in my soul what evil is, deeper than you'll ever know. I know evil when I see it, and I done cast it out of me!" Jimson Weed said with the conviction of a jackleg preacher in a storefront church.

"I don't know what evil is, but I do know one thing. I want that baby and I want her today," I said as patiently as I could. Suddenly, I was sick and tired of these two and this discussion on the nature of evil. "I know the baby was here, and I need to talk to Thelma Lee. If Thelma Lee changed her mind, that's fine. But if I haven't heard from her by six p.m. tonight, and Treyman Barnes doesn't have his grand-child, I am going to report it to the police."

I knew I was on shaky legal ground. Technically, Thelma Lee could have been accused of kidnapping the moment she snatched the child, and the moment I agreed to try to get the child from her, some wily prosecutor could accuse me of aiding and abetting. But Jimson and Sweet Thing didn't strike me as legal hounds. The bad thing was, I was beginning to have second thoughts about the ethics of taking Barnes's check and my role in all this. The good thing was, I didn't have to worry because Barnes was as connected to the powers that be and the legal establishment as Carmela Soprano was to the mob.

They glanced at each other and then back at me.

"Get the hell out of here," Jimson said with nothing in his eyes but hatred, which puzzled me.

"Well, I hope you two are ready for what comes next," I said quietly.

"It can't be nothing worse than what I seen," said Jimson, and the look in his eyes made me a believer. I handed Sweet Thing another card.

"I already got one," she said.

"Take another."

Jimson snatched it from her, tore it up, and threw it on the floor. He went back into the kitchen, slamming the door behind him.

"He don't mean no harm," Sweet Thing said as soon as he'd left.

"Ever since he come into my life, after my sweet Lily died, all he ever wanted to do was love me and protect me and keep evil people from hurting me. Sometimes I think he loves me more than is good for him. You ever have a man love you like that?" she asked. Her eyes filled with tears, and she glanced away so I wouldn't see them.

"No, I can't say that I have." I wondered who this Lily was she was talking about, but the tears kept me from asking. Lilah's namesake, I assumed.

When I heard the sound of bacon sizzling, I gave her another card.

"I don't want to see Thelma Lee in jail any more than you do, and I want what's best for the baby," I whispered. "Please call me if you need to."

She nodded that she would, then folded the card twice and stuck it in her bosom.

I DROVE AROUND THE BLOCK and parked close enough to keep an eye on the house but far enough away not to be noticed. I put on some CDs and, when I got sick of those, an audiobook. Thelma Lee was bound to come home sooner or later, I figured, and I wanted to see what had happened.

I waited for nearly four hours, then started calling Treyman Barnes. The first few times, the receptionist said he'd call me back when he returned, then he began sending my calls straight to voice mail. Finally, I got mad. The least he could do was return my damn calls.

The way I figured it, though, was that Barnes had taken care of things in his own way. He'd probably decided he didn't want a third person involved and called Thelma Lee and arranged to meet her himself. More than likely, he'd given her some cash and taken the baby home. If they went to court, there would be one less person involved. It would be quick, clean, with no witnesses, the way Barnes probably liked it.

What Barnes knew that Lilah and her relatives didn't was that the parent who has the child usually gets to keep her. Lilah's mistake was not screaming "kidnap" from the get. There wasn't a judge in Jersey who would favor Lilah Love's right to her baby over that of Barnes's son, and his being a vet would make it all the easier. Lilah Love would probably never see that child again.

But why was Thelma Lee so scared?

I left Treyman Barnes a final message when I got back to my office: "Mr. Barnes, since I haven't heard from you, I assume you've been in touch with the party we discussed last night and that the two of you have come to an agreement regarding your granddaughter. If that's the case, then our business is concluded. Your retainer was sufficient for my brief service. I'll mail you an invoice and a full report for your records. Thank you again, and I hope I can be of service in the future."

Then you working for the Devil! Jimson Weed's voice mocked me, but I pushed it back.

I peeked into the Beauty Biscuit on my way home from work that night, but Wyvetta wasn't there. I'd check in with her tomorrow. It had been a long day, and I was eager to see Jamal; we had some making up to do.

"How about some Red Lobster tonight?" I yelled as I walked into the house, determined to start the night off right. I checked my messages one last time to see if I'd heard from Barnes, but there was nothing.

"Come on, Jamal, I'm hungry! I want to get on the road before it gets too late," I yelled again as I sorted through the usual mess of bills and mail.

The doorbell rang twice, and I went to answer it, tossing the unwanted junk in the kitchen trash on the way to the door. "Come on down, Jamal, I'll be in the car," I said, grabbing my bag off the back of a chair and heading out. I'd get rid of whoever it was as quick as I could; the thought of Chardonnay and Cajun shrimp was making my stomach growl. I stopped short when I looked through the peephole.

Two of them were standing there, one white, one black; one older and shorter by three inches, both clean shaven, neatly dressed, one in gray, the other in blue. No style. Cheap suits. I knew the look: stare straight ahead, no show of feelings, hands at side, never let them see what's on your mind. I cracked the door, left the chain on.

The older one spoke first, pulling out a badge as if I needed to see one. I'd been a cop myself once.

"Is this the residence of Jamal Curtis?" The question was simply put, with no threat, no assumption made. Professional. I gave him that.

I nodded, unable to speak. Finally, I got the words out. "I'm Jamal's mother. Has something happened?"

"I'm Detective Ransom, and this is Detective Coates. We'd like to speak to him," said the young one. He was well built and blond, his hair circling his head in a wreath of golden curls. A rookie Adonis, smug and sure of himself for no good reason.

What could they possibly want with my son? I tried to send Jamal a message. *Don't come down, Son. Don't come down!* I kept my eyes glued to the young cop's face. "He's not home from school yet," I said.

"School?"

"Summer school."

"It's going on six. Kind of late, isn't it? From what I remember, summer schools end at noon," Ransom said. A smart-ass. I saw that by the way he looked me over, chin jutting out.

"What do you want to talk to my son about?" I knew the deal with cops and black boys. Pull them over first. Ask questions later. Shoot before they answer sometimes. Always the suspect. Always the victim.

"May we come in?" Coates asked, his voice patient, polite.

Don't let them in. I knew that instinctively.

Coates was old enough to have known my brother, one of that first wave of young black men who had joined the force to make a difference in the lives of the black community. But his weary eyes told me that the world he patrolled had worn him down; he was probably ready to retire, bounce grandkids on his knee, and never think about what he'd seen.

"I was just on my way out." I stepped onto the porch, slamming the door behind me. The younger one threw a furtive glance at the older, who stared straight ahead. "What do you want with my son?"

"We need to ask him about something he may have seen." The rookie's gaze and tone were cocksure. I know how to handle this bitch, that look said, but the older one shifted his eyes from me to the rookie; the slight flick of an eyebrow said he'd take it over.

Jake. His name came to me as it always did when there is trouble with Jamal. *Don't let them talk to Jamal unless Jake is present.* "Just what do you think he saw?"

"We're investigating a murder that occurred last night. We have reason to believe that your son may have been with the victim prior to the murder or may even have been one of the last people to see the victim alive. We found an item that belonged to your son in her car."

"Her?" The question in my voice told them more than I wanted them to know.

"Perhaps you knew her," the veteran said. "The victim's name was Lilah Love. She was brutally beaten to death late last night. We found her body in the trunk of her rented Altima at seven thirty this morning."

"When was the last time you saw your son?" The young one shot his question out, his eyes recording everything that flitted across my face.

"When I took him to school this morning," I lied with everything I had.

Coates gave me his card. "Please call us when your son gets home tonight. He may have witnessed the murder or seen the killer."

"Or had something to do with the crime," the rookie added.

HERE IS MY SON?

I drove around the block like a crazy woman, then parked on a parallel street and waited to see if the cops were still there. I was shaking so hard, I couldn't dial my boy's cell number. Finally, I did and there was no answer, of course. I called the house again, hoping he had snuck in without my knowing it or fallen asleep, and when nobody answered, I sat there like a fool listening to my own voice telling me I wasn't home.

Where the hell did he go?

In case the two cops were still lurking around, I grabbed a dirty raincoat I'd stuffed in my trunk, walked around the block, then snuck in through my back door like a thief, hoping my neighbors wouldn't call the police.

"Jamal!" I wailed, even though I knew he wasn't there. I ran into his room, then stood in the middle of the floor trying to calm myself down. He must have left something, somewhere. I turned on the light and sank down on the bed trying to remember what was in its place and what was missing. The Nets backpack Jake had bought him last fall was on the back of the chair where he always hung it. I rifled through it, not sure what I was looking for, and found nothing. A sheet of homework had fallen on the floor next to the chair with yesterday's date on it. Had he even gone to school today? Had he gone and come back? Hotshot PI couldn't find her own kid.

The bed was neatly made. Late-rising Jamal never had time to make it in the morning; usually, he pulled the sheets up right before he climbed into bed at night. The sheet and blanket were tucked in tight, hospital cornered like my brother had taught me to do, like I had taught Jamal.

What were the last words I said to him?

Stay mad. I love you anyway.

Would they haunt me forever?

I searched his closet, frantically tossing clothes on the floor, looking for nothing and everything. Sneakers. (More pairs than he'd need in a decade.) T-shirts. (Where the hell did these wife-beaters come from?) A month's worth of dirty drawers and socks stuffed in a pillowcase. (How had I raised such a pig?) I smiled at that, then cried, then made myself focus again. *What was missing?* Dress slacks, the beautiful sweater I'd bought him last fall. Remembering how he loved it brought more tears. But why had he taken it in the middle of the summer? What had he been thinking?

I went through the top of his closet searching for his duffel bag, the one I'd ordered from L.L.Bean when he'd gone to that computer camp, the one with his initials embroidered on it, the one I couldn't find. The cops hadn't said what they'd found in Lilah's car, but that had to be it. It had two sets of labels—name, address, telephone number on them—when I'd sent him off to camp, every bit of information a person would need to find him.

If you want to live with your jackass of a father, then go right ahead and do it!

I called DeWayne, but there was no answer, so I left a message at his home and on his cell phone, telling him to call me back. He occasionally traveled during the week, so I wasn't surprised he wasn't home. He was also of that generation that left their cell phones off. Eventually, he'd check for messages. I didn't say why I'd called, that Jamal wasn't here. I didn't want to hear his mouth about the way I was raising his son.

Damn him to hell!

Was he right?

I ran downstairs and snatched a list with the telephone numbers of Jamal's friends off the refrigerator. I left messages for the boys I knew he hung with even though it wasn't quite nine. No teenager worth the name would be home now. Surprisingly, I got two of his friends, one home sick, the other on punishment. No, they hadn't seen him since yesterday when they played ball in the park. No, they didn't know where he'd gone. Yes, they would call me if they heard from him. Did you check his webpage? one asked.

Webpage?

I turned on Jamal's computer and went to his browser to check the sites he'd visited. MySpace.com was at the top of the list. I certainly knew what MySpace was but had never visited it; figured it was for kids and politicians trying to get a vote. Jamal's name came up on the MySpace page requesting his password. "Remember Me" had not been checked.

Password?

I tried his name spelled backward, then *DeWayne, Jake, Snoop Doggy Dogg, Beyoncé, Frosty,* his beloved deceased guinea pig. I tried *50 Cent, Cent 50, Beyoncé* spelled backward, then random words—*thug, cash, popcorn shrimp.* Then, considering all the shit he'd been through in the past year, the boy he had loved more than anyone else and whose death had begun his relationship with violent death—his half brother Hakim, shot down in front of him ten years ago.

Bingo.

A photo of Jamal standing tall and handsome holding a basketball popped up. Music boomed, some rap song I couldn't understand, and the words "Tell Me About Yourself" appeared on the right side of the page. He'd answered every damn question.

Name —	Jamal
Birth Date —	October 3
Place —	The Little Orange, not to be confused with the Big Apple
Eye Color —	Black
Race —	African American
Preference —	Straight
Preference in Partners —	Sexy women who like to do it

What?!

Looking for —	Joy and happiness
Fear —	Death by gun
Favorite Color —	Blue
Favorite Restaurant —	Friday's

What happened to Red Lobster?

Favorite Sport — Lifting weights, capoeira

I scrolled down his webpage, stunned by how much he had revealed about himself. I searched for recent comments. My mouth dropped open when I read them:

NEED TO GET DA FUCK OUTTA HERE. FAST.
can a pretty woman slide through here and
pick me up? No strings attached.

No strings attached! What the hell did he mean by that? Had he lost his mind putting something like that on the Web? Didn't he know a site like this was Pedophile Central for any horny pervert who wanted to take a peek? He might think he was all big and bad with his new muscles and martial arts skills, but they wouldn't count for shit against a cloth filled with chloroform. Any ole crazy person with his name and ZIP code could look him up.

And one ole crazy person had. "Aunt Lilah" in pretty lime green script had stepped out of the shadows and answered his request.

met you today. Friend of your mama's, but I can keep
a secret. I'm out of here late tonight. I need to get
out of town for a couple of days. company sound
real good about now. especially with a fine young
thing like you! give me a call, we'll set something up.

Take it easy, girl! Just breathe and take it easy! I told myself, and that was just what I did for the next five minutes, rocking back and forth in my baby's chair, inhaling and exhaling until I got hold of myself. The cops had it right. Jamal had been with her. But where was she taking him? Where she wanted to go or where he did? Where was he now?

I called Jake out of habit, left a hysterical message, then remembered he was at a conference in Toronto. I was about to leave a message on his cell phone, then realized there was absolutely nothing he could do in Canada, so I hung up. I tried DeWayne again; he sure had the right to know what was going on now. No answer. He was bound to be there sooner or later. I knew I'd go crazy if I just sat here staring at that computer. Better to get on the road, figure out what to do on the way down to DeWayne's. Jamal had a key, and even if his father wasn't home, he might still be there. If he was, I'd be able to sleep tonight. If not, best to tell his daddy in person so we could figure out our next move together. I tossed a change of clothes, a robe, and a toothbrush into an overnight bag, ran down the street to where I'd parked my car, and sped down the parkway. DeWayne kept a spare set of house keys under a planter on his back porch, so if nobody was there, I'd spend the night and head back home tomorrow morning.

I couldn't get Lilah Love out of my mind. What else did the cops know about her? Did they know about the money she'd given me? Did they think I was involved in her death, that maybe my son had been doing my bidding? And truth be told, if I'd known about the moves she'd made on my son, I would have beaten the woman to death myself.

Who could have done it? Who had the most to gain? Down how many dark alleys had she switched that skinny little butt? That Turk guy skulking around with his tail between his legs was a keeper. Thieves have no loyalty, and a thieving dog will rip out a master's throat as quick as he'll lick her hand. Lilah had mentioned something about Turk working for some big-time gangster gone legit. Was she talking about Treyman Barnes? He would gain from Lilah's death. But why bother if he already had the baby? Revenge maybe? Just plain nastiness?

I pulled into DeWayne's driveway at midnight feeling like I'd driven the whole way without taking a breath. I sat in the car for ten minutes thinking of what I'd say to DeWayne if Jamal wasn't there. If the situation were reversed, there would be no end to my rage. I'd curse him out so bad his granddaddy would turn over in his grave.

The sudden, sharp rap on the window made me jump so high I hit my head on the ceiling, then banged my elbow on the steering wheel as I scrambled out of the car. And I didn't feel a damn thing.

SEVEN

"WHERE HAVE YOU BEEN, JAMAL? Where have you been?" I wailed like a kid, grabbed my son, and held him tightly.

"He's been down here with me. Where you think he's been?" said an indignant DeWayne. Releasing Jamal, I jumped in DeWayne's face.

"What the hell is wrong with you, DeWayne Curtis? Why don't you join the twenty-first century and keep on your damn cell phone? Do you know what I've been going through up there? Did he tell you what happened? Have you lost your fuck—"

"Mom." Jamal placed himself between me and his father. "It's not his fault. I only told him you didn't know where I was a couple of hours ago. Don't blame him!"

I glanced at my watch, then at my son. "Then let me blame you! Do you know what time it is? It's midnight! I had my cell on while I drove. I left a dozen messages on your cell. Do you think I pay my hard-earned money to Verizon Wireless every month for the hell of it?"

"Let's go in the house, sit down, and sort this mess out," DeWayne said, interrupting me in the sanest voice I'd heard in years. "Come on, Tammy, I'll get you a drink. You look like shit."

Silently, the three of us settled around the kitchen table like some sitcom version of a happy family. DeWayne's kitchen was small and neat, the shiny stove, refrigerator, and dishwasher hinting that they were rarely if ever used. I recognized the blue Formica table as one that had belonged to his grandmother; that was one thing he hadn't changed. It was wobbly and narrow; I pulled my knees in so they wouldn't touch his.

It had been years since I'd sat across from my ex-husband, and every feeling I'd ever had about him swept through me in a miserable rush. First came bitterness about his countless betrayals, and disgust at how easily he'd fooled me, then, unexpectedly, a gentler emotion—recognition of his love for our son. If there was one thing in De-Wayne's wretched world that made sense to him, it was Jamal, and I had to respect him for that. He would give his life for this boy as quickly and unquestionably as I would mine.

This was his son, there was no mistaking that. His eyes were the long-lashed ones of his father, which could charm an uncharmable woman with a wink. He had DeWayne's build, and seeing the two of them together reminded me of what I'd once loved about the man. His voice had grown deep like DeWayne's even though it kept the easy rhythm of my brother's.

"How about a drink?" DeWayne said, bringing me from my thoughts. "Should be some of that red wine Shelia left in the wine cellar when she split."

"So Shelia left you?" DeWayne had been involved with so many women for so many years, I'd stopped keeping count. According to Jamal, Shelia was the latest and the best. She was about my age, which made her ten years younger than DeWayne, smart and classy, with a PhD in English from Rutgers and a pedigree from a family tree of New Brunswick doctors. DeWayne had wooed and won her as he had so many others—with his *GQ* good looks and the sharpest wheels in town. But I noticed with some satisfaction that he was beginning to show his age. His eyelids had a droop, and his dull skin hinted of too much good scotch gulped down with too many fast women.

"Yeah. They all leave me sooner or later, don't they, Tammy?"

"If you call me Tammy again, I'm going to stab you through the ear," I said; I was in that kind of mood. He actually looked scared for a moment, then chuckled.

"All that time we were married, you'd think I'd remember by now, don't you?"

It had been the eyes that had gotten me, that lazy smile that promised a woman more loving than she'd ever had before. I'd found out the truth of that pretty damn fast.

"Another one gone, huh?" I couldn't resist it.

"You're still my favorite."

"Mom," Jamal warned, spotting the loathing that flashed in my eyes.

"Let me get you that wine, Tamara." DeWayne saw it, too, and headed out of the kitchen and down into the basement. When he was gone, I hugged Jamal again, and my eyes filled with tears.

"I'm sorry, Mom. I just didn't know what else to do. Everything happened so fast, I knew you were mad at me, and—"

"Do you know the police are looking for you? They came by the house."

"Cops? Why are they looking for me? I didn't do nothing!"

"Lilah Love is dead, Jamal. Somebody beat her to death."

He didn't move but looked straight ahead as the terror gradually overcame him, beginning in his eyes, traveling down to his trembling lips, then down to his young, broad shoulders. I got out of my chair and held him, big as he was, like he was my little boy again.

"What happened, Ma? What happened? Why would that person kill her?"

I stopped and studied his face. "Why would *what person* kill her?"

"The person who got into the car with her, the person she said she was picking up! Why would somebody kill her? She wasn't going to do anything to anybody, she was really nice, and she—"

"You don't know what that bitch was capable of doing," I said, angry at him all over again for getting into the car to begin with. "What in the hell is wrong with you? How could you risk your life like that? Why would you—"

"Stop yelling at the boy and let him tell you what happened!" De-Wayne interrupted me as he strode into the room with an attitude and a bottle of wine. "You yelling at the boy ain't going to do no good. Did I hear you say something about the police?"

"They came to the house tonight."

"About what?" he eyed me suspiciously.

"About a woman who was murdered, the one who was going to bring him down here."

Fear was in DeWayne's face now, too. "Was that the woman who you said didn't come back, your mama's friend?" DeWayne asked

Jamal, throwing me a dirty look, but his eyes softened as he sat down. "We in this together, Tamara, you know that as well as me. We got to take care of this together."

This sudden talk of togetherness made me sick, but he was right, so I nodded in agreement. I took a sip of the wine, then damn near choked when I noticed the glass it was in. It was part of a set of crystal ones I'd bought the last year we were together. At least three had been hurled at him from across the room, the first when I found out he was sleeping with his secretary.

"Only one left, saved it for you. I'll break it when you leave," DeWayne joked. He always did like to play with fire.

"Here, let me do it for you." I swallowed the wine in a single gulp and hurled the glass hard against the far wall above the sink. It shattered, leaving a blood-red stain over the lemon yellow kitchen wall. I thought about how the Barnes kid had thrown that ashtray across the room and was ashamed that I'd let this fool get the better of me.

"Feeling better?" said DeWayne, the "mature" adult.

Jamal looked from him to me, and his eyes got big like they used to get when we fought and he was a little boy.

"I'm sorry about that. My nerves are really shot," I said, and meant it.

He shrugged. "No harm done. This has been a bad night for all of us." He got the broom and dustpan, swept up the glass, and sat back down. I reached across the table and took Jamal's hand.

"Start it from the beginning, baby. Right after we had that fight."

"Fight? You had a fight? No wonder the boy left!" DeWayne reared back in protective papa mode.

"Shut up and listen," I said. He glanced at Jamal and took my advice.

"When I logged on after I went upstairs, I—"

"Logged on? What's he talking about?" DeWayne's puzzled gaze clearly revealed his age, proving he was even more ignorant about computers than me.

"Then I surfed the Web for a while and came back to my page when I got a message from Miss Love. From Lilah to something I had written," Jamal continued.

" 'Need to get da fuck outta here. Fast,' " I said.

Jamal covered his face, "Mom, I didn't know . . ."

"Do you think I was born yesterday?"

"What the fuck is he talking about, writing something like that, using language like that? What the fuck kind of boy did you raise—" DeWayne sputtered on. I ignored him, and Jamal continued.

"So she wrote me an answer to what I, you know, said and said she'd pick me up if I called her, so I did."

"What time did you call her?"

"While you were in the tub. She said she'd pick me up near the house at one a.m. and she'd give me a ride wherever I wanted to go. So when I knew you were asleep, I climbed out my window and pulled the shade down so you wouldn't know it was up. I didn't want to risk going downstairs—you know that stair that creaks? The roof from my window is low, and it's not that far from the ground. I just jumped down into the backyard."

"So what did she say when you got in the car?"

"Said she was going to Atlantic City, and she could drop me off on the way. At my dad's place. Said she'd like to meet him anyway, since she knew you and everything."

"Now *that* would have been a match straight from hell," I muttered. "Go on, Son."

"She was real nice, like she was in your office, and she said she was your friend, and—"

"Didn't you teach my son never to talk to strangers?" DeWayne's face filled with paternal outrage.

"Didn't you?" I shot back.

"He lives with you."

"You both did," Jamal said, pleading for peace. "I knew that. When I was a kid, you *both* told me. I know not to talk to strangers, I know never to get in a stranger's car, but she wasn't exactly a stranger. I met her in your office, Mom. And anyway, look at me. I'm not a kid anymore. I outweighed her by about a hundred pounds. I know how to fight; I know how to take care of myself." He stiffened his back he-man style, and all I could do was sigh.

"Not if there's some nigger in the backseat with a gun at the back of your head," DeWayne said.

"I'm not stupid, Dad," Jamal said, raising his voice slightly. "I checked the backseat before I got in. I looked around good before I threw in my bag. I knew she was alone, and I thought I could handle it, and I could have, if she hadn't gotten that call."

"What call?" DeWayne and I asked in unison.

"I told you, somebody called her."

"Tell me everything you can remember about that," I said. "Tell me how her voice sounded, exactly what she said to the person."

"We were heading to the turnpike, and Lilah got this call on her cell. She got real mad, and she kept arguing with whoever it was and said it was nobody's business what she did with what was hers. Then she started laughing and turned around and headed back to Newark. She pulled onto Raymond Boulevard, then pulled over to the side and called somebody else."

"Did she say anybody's name?"

Jamal thought for a moment. "No. She just dialed a number, then she said, 'Guess who I'm talking to in half a minute. Yeah, that's who it is, and it's about you know what, too. What else we got to talk about?' She laughed again and hung up. Then she pulled over to the side and told me to get out."

"Told you to get out?" DeWayne asked.

"She said, 'I got to take care of this before I leave town,' and she nodded toward someone who was standing far away on the corner. She said she'd swing back around the block, then pick me up in about fifteen minutes when she was through."

"Did the person see you?"

"Yeah, I guess so. I don't know who it was because he was too far away to see his face."

"How do you know it was a man?"

"I *don't* know, Mom, I really don't know!"

"Then it could have been a woman?"

"Yeah. I don't know!"

"So what happened next?" I asked.

"She picked the person up, and she drove away. I waited for her for about an hour, then I walked to Penn Station and I got some money out of the ATM, then I waited for a bus so I could come down here."

"Did anybody see you or talk to you?" I said, hoping he had some kind of alibi.

"No, I just sat there waiting on the corner, then I walked to Penn Station, and that was all."

"Jamal, why didn't you call me?" I couldn't keep the cry out of my voice.

"I was afraid you'd be mad." He shook his head wearily and sighed. "Mom, I'm sorry she's dead. Maybe I should have stayed, maybe—"

"Never mind about Lilah Love. You better start worrying about your own silly behind. You left your duffel bag with all those tags in the backseat of the woman's car. That's how the cops knew you were there and how to find you. The police and anybody else who might be looking for you, if they couldn't figure it out from all that dumb stuff you left on MySpace."

"I didn't put my address on MySpace. Everybody writes dumb stuff on MySpace," Jamal said lamely.

"You put down your name, and anybody typing in your ZIP code could get to your page quick. That's how Lilah found you."

"MySpace? What's he talking about MySpace? What do you mean he left some dumb stuff on MySpace?" asked DeWayne.

"It's computer stuff, Dad," Jamal said in a tone that said they'd had that conversation before.

"What time did you get the bus?" I said, ignoring DeWayne.

"I waited around in Penn Station and took the first bus I could to Atlantic City. I guess around noon. It was a local, so it took a long time."

"He called me from the bus stop. I brought him here. He took a shower, had a nap, I got him a toothbrush and some more clothes, and then we went out to Friday's. That's his favorite spot, you know," said DeWayne with smug certainty.

"Friday's?" I asked, and Jamal gave me a guilty glance.

"That's where he told me what happened. He didn't know about anybody being killed. It's a shame about that woman, isn't it? Where do you know her from?" asked DeWayne.

"Jamaica. A long time ago."

"Jamaica? You must have been down there with that damned Basil Dupre. I should have known he had something to do with this shit. I blame that son of a bitch for breaking up our marriage, Tammy. I blame that bastard—"

I threw him a look that shut him up quick. He finished his wine and poured himself some scotch. Straight. "So what we going to do about this here mess?" he said.

Jamal yawned, collapsing his head in his hands.

"Go on to bed, Son, and your father and I will talk to you in the morning," I said. Jamal kissed me good night and headed upstairs.

"He better stay down here with me until this mess blows over," DeWayne said as soon as he was out of earshot, and I agreed. "What else do you think we should do?"

"I'll go back tomorrow and see what else I can find out," I said.

"Don't you have some lawyer-friend up there who can handle this?"

"He won't be back until Monday, and I don't know how to get in touch with him."

"We can't wait until then," DeWayne said, shaking his head. "I got a friend I can call. A lawyer. Handled my last divorce. I'll talk to her in the morning." He yawned twice and stretched. "Well, I'm going to hit the sack, too. The couch in the study lets down into a reasonably comfortable bed, Tammy. I'll go upstairs and get you some clean sheets."

"No, *you* sleep on the damned couch in the damned study, and get me some sheets for that California king-size bed you got upstairs," I corrected him. "I want some comfort, some privacy, and you out of my face."

He looked hurt for a moment, then obediently climbed the stairs and got the sheets I'd requested.

I settled into his bed, every bone and muscle aching. But I had one more thing to do. I had to talk to a good friend, who I hadn't spoken to in a month of Sundays. Her name was Matilda Gilroy, a cop in Belvington Heights, where I used to work. When I quit, they hired Matilda to fill the "woman" quota. We'd been friends ever since, and the fact that she was white didn't change our friendship one bit. We both loved Sleepytime tea, had grown up poor, and been married to jerks. Our sons were about the same age, too. A couple years back, her son, Jeremy, had run away, and I'd found him and brought him home safe. She said she owed me big for that, and to call her anytime day or night if I ever needed anything. I needed it now.

"Matilda Gilroy here," she said when she answered the phone. She was always business—at work, at home, in bed—and I smiled as her image came to mind. She was beanpole thin with a bony, narrow face that had never met a blusher it didn't like. Her lank hair had been every shade of blonde there was, and her large, able hands, which never seemed to rest, were always topped by short nails painted some bright tropical color. Matilda Gilroy, bless her soul, was one of the oddest-looking women I'd ever known; she also had the biggest heart.

"Hey, Matty, it's me, Tamara Hayle."

"Tamara Hayle! What are you doing calling me at this time of night? Jamal okay?" she asked in the same breath.

"Barely. He had a close call with the boys, and I need you to get me some information."

She coughed, and I heard her light a cigarette. "Our boys? Belvington Heights? They better get their shit together."

"No. My town this time. They found a dead body in the trunk of a rented car this morning. A woman named Lilah Love. Can you get me some information on it?"

"They think Jamal is mixed up with that?!"

"I don't know what they think, to tell you the truth, but get me what you can, okay?"

"You know I will, Tam." She paused for a moment. "Every time I look at my son, I say a prayer for you."

"Thanks, Matty."

"First thing tomorrow morning I'll look into it. I know somebody over there who owes me a favor, so I should be able to get something for you soon. Now I'm going back to sleep, okay?" She hung up before I could answer. I sank into DeWayne's pillow of a bed and went out fast.

Matty was on the case. She called me back in the morning before I had brushed my teeth.

Lilah hadn't been beaten like the cops had said, Matty told me. She'd been killed quickly and brutally: a fist driven straight through her throat, crushing her larynx back against itself like it was nothing. They suspected it was somebody she knew—unless it was a professional, which seemed unlikely; only folks you knew killed you like that. They liked this guy named Turk Orlando for the killing and were looking for him.

I thanked Matty for the information, shook my head, and sighed.

So my girl Lilah died just like she lived—fast and mean.

T WAS A LONG WAY HOME, and I felt every mile. My back hurt, my head ached, and I couldn't stop worrying about Jamal. Why had he gotten into that woman's car in the first place? Had he been so angry at me, so mistrustful of sharing his feelings, that he forgot every rule I'd ever taught him? Yeah, he was almost a man—or thought he was—but why had he acted so impulsively? I answered my questions even as I asked them. Because of those murders in my city, the deaths of so many kids his age. They made him reckless, careless. A confrontation with violent death could make you do strange things. My first year on the force had made me fearful and anxious, jumping at my own shadow. Jamal was flirting with danger, defying it, and that scared the hell out of me. How much more would he risk?

I wondered if Lilah Love had told him about our activities down in Jamaica. I could almost hear that whiny voice sharing my involvement in her sordid little tale. The thought that had worried me when she first walked into my office hit me again. Did she have something on me? Could I be tied to her murder?

I couldn't cut the memory of Lilah's murder loose. How do you jam a fist through a woman's throat? Shooting somebody I can almost understand. Banging somebody over the head, well, depends on the circumstances. But balling your fist and slamming it so hard into flesh that you kill somebody? That was a special kind of brutality, a special kind of killer.

The cops would be looking for someone with a lot of rage and huge fists. That would be Turk. But thanks to his anger over all the murders in town and his martial arts training, that might also be my son, who, as far as they knew, was the last person to see Lilah alive, which could make him a prime suspect. At the very least, he was a material witness. The good thing was they hadn't gone down to South Jersey to pick him up. The bad thing was they could take their own sweet time. Jamal's duffel bag was hard evidence if they needed it. He wouldn't be completely beyond suspicion until they found out who really did it.

Lilah had treated Turk like a homeless mutt, and he had probably turned on her like one. You can't order a grown man around like she had Monday in my office and not expect some kind of payback. Another possibility was the emotionally fragile Barnes kid. I wondered if the cops knew about him. She could have been referring to their child when she said "it was nobody's business what she did with what was hers." Pure and simple rage could have made Troy Barnes snap and hit her with the same force with which he'd smashed that glass ashtray on his daddy's wall. He was a trained killer, according to Lilah, and if that was true, he knew half a dozen ways to kill somebody with his bare hands. Or maybe somebody else killed her, some man Lilah had picked up on a whim. Somebody she owed money to or who owed money to her. Someone she had something on. Somebody like me, the cops might say.

What else we got to talk about?

The person on the other end would know what that something was and who she was about to meet.

Guess who I'm talking to in half a minute.

Anybody could have killed her. Anybody but me or my boy.

I'd eaten a late breakfast with Jamal when he got up and held him until he got embarrassed and squirmed to get loose. He grinned when I told him that summer school would have to come later, and I'd been glad to see that grin. Then I got on the road. That was all I could do, except keep my ears and eyes open and see what the day would bring.

I didn't feel like going home. Nothing waited for me there but a sink full of dishes and a whole lot of worry, so I headed straight to my office. At least, I could water my plant. At best, I could make some notes about my last meeting with Lilah Love.

I got to get back something that belongs to me. Something important. Stolen property, you might say.

If Lilah considered Baby Dal "property," she could be sold to anybody who wanted to buy her, and that had been Treyman Barnes, or so he'd told me.

But who had the baby now?

Thelma Lee, as far as I knew.

If Thelma Lee had given—or sold—the baby to Treyman Barnes yesterday morning when she was supposed to meet me, could *he* have gone after Lilah to make sure she was out of the picture once and for all? There would be no legal challenges then, that was for sure. But he

wouldn't have done it himself. More than likely he'd have had somebody do it for him. Somebody like Turk. But why would Treyman
Barnes go that far?

I don't give a shit about the law. There are ways around the law.

And one of those ways was murder.

It was still early when I pulled into the lot across from my building.
I'd had coffee with breakfast but could use another cup, so I stopped
in the café that had recently opened across the street and got a double.
I peeked into the Biscuit on the way upstairs to see if Wyvetta was
around and spotted her in the back getting ready for her day. I thought
about dropping in to tell her what was going on, but gossip buzzes
around Wyvetta like flies around molasses. Wyvetta was as quick to
gossip as she was to listen. Best to keep my business to myself.

I should have noticed the long, pretty Benz parked in front of my
building. Standing the way it was between a beat-up Ford and a dirty
Honda, it glittered in the sun like a pile of silver dollars. But I just
didn't think about it until the owner stomped into my office and
parked his plump little butt in the chair across from me.

"What the fuck is going on?" said Treyman Barnes, fast, loud, and
in my face.

Stunned, I sat there, coffee cup midway between lip and chin.

"I want to know what the fuck is going on!"

Had this jackass lost his natural mind?

I carefully placed my cup down, gave a ladylike blot to my lips
with a napkin, and smiled sweetly. "Good morning, Mr. Barnes. What
can I do for you today?" That bullshit little greeting took everything
I had.

"You can do what the fuck I paid you that thousand dollars to do, that's what! You can bring me that baby like you said you would! Or are you holding out for more like I think you are?"

It took a full minute for me to gather my thoughts and my cool.

"I did what the *fuck* you hired me to do," I said, tossing him back what he'd tossed me. He narrowed his eyes, trying to scare somebody, and he did—me.

"I want that child," he said.

"As far as I'm concerned, you've got that child, so get your sorry ass out of my office." I took a swallow of coffee, praying I wouldn't choke.

He stepped back, took a breath, then gave me the charming, cherubic grin he probably bestowed on folks before he ripped out their throats.

"We've gotten off on the wrong foot this morning, haven't we, Ms. Hayle? Forgive me. I sometimes forget I'm not talking to some of those hardheads who come my way and that I'm in the presence of a lady. I had to make sure of something. Understand where you were coming from. May we start again? Please?"

I waited a beat, then, with a curt nod, indicated that I would give him another chance.

"Do you know where my grandchild is?"

"I assumed you had her. Didn't you get my message concerning Thelma Lee Sweets?"

He hesitated. "Yes, I did. I thought it best if I talked to her myself, so I called her shortly after I got your message."

"Late Monday night?"

"Yes. She said she would bring the baby to my office first thing on

Tuesday morning. I waited around until late, but she didn't show up. Then she called me around five, said she wanted to meet me at this motel off the highway, this shit hole of a place on the edge of town. I hated to think of her taking my grandchild to a place like that. Why she'd want to meet me there I have no idea, but she insisted, and I said I would. But I didn't know whether she'd bother to show up this time or not, and I'd canceled too many appointments already, so I told her it would be late."

"How late?"

"I told her eight, then she said it would have to be later than that. I heard somebody in the background then, a man, yelling at her, arguing with her. He wanted me to come even later, and they wanted some money. I heard that because she got back on and told me to come at midnight and bring some cash. She hadn't asked for money before, so I figured she got herself a partner. Then I heard the baby crying, so I knew they had her. They asked for fifty thousand dollars in cash, and that's what I got out."

"Fifty thousand? Just like that?" I didn't hide my amazement both that Thelma had the nerve to ask and that he'd had it on hand.

"I keep a lot of cash in my safe. Unexpected costs sometimes arise," he said impatiently. "I went to where she said, but she wasn't there. Never showed up. I knocked hard on the door, but the room was locked. I remember that filthy place from years ago. Made me uncomfortable. I didn't want to be seen there or stay around. I figured maybe she changed her mind again, and because you knew what was going on, knew how much I wanted the baby, I figured maybe you—"

"You thought I had something to do with this?" My throat was so tight with anger, I could barely speak.

He glanced away quickly and then looked straight at me. "Yeah, I didn't know. I thought maybe you'd tried to cut some kind of a deal with her, include yourself in it. That's why I came in here yelling about the baby. I wanted to see your reaction. I figured you'd ask for the money. But you passed the test."

I sat for a minute, too mad to respond, then said, "Are you aware that Lilah Love was murdered Monday night? They found her body Tuesday morning in her rented car. Maybe Thelma Lee didn't come because she just found out about her sister." I threw it out quickly, studying *him* for a reaction, seeing if he'd pass *my* test.

He stared back hard, gave me nothing, passed with flying colors. "So Lilah Love is dead? She got what she deserved," he said.

Could Treyman Barnes be the "big-time gangster who done gone legit" Lilah had said Turk worked for? "Do you know a man named Turk Orlando?" I asked.

"I know a lot of men named Turk, and one city named Orlando," he said with a smart-ass grin.

"Cops are looking for him."

"You think I give a damn?"

I took a breath, let it out. "So what do you want from me now?"

"Thelma Lee is Lilah Love's sister. She must still have the baby. So I want you to find Thelma Lee."

"Again?"

"Again," he said. "You know where she is, don't you?"

"I have no idea, but if I did, do you think I'd tell you so you can get some hardhead to shove a fist into her throat like he did her sister?" The words tumbled out before I knew I'd said them or thought good about how he'd take them; he didn't take them well. His grin slid downward into an ugly grimace that brought out the cruelty in his eyes. Then he changed up quickly, smiled, pulled out his checkbook, started to write.

You be careful around Treyman Barnes, you hear me, Tamara?

"I don't want your money, Mr. Barnes," I said, suddenly as wary of him as Wyvetta had warned me to be. "My calendar is full now, and I'm simply not able to help you. I will type up my report, and you will receive it in the mail by the end of the week. If, after reading it, you'd like your money refunded, I'll gladly do it, and if you have any problems with that, please take them up with the state agency. I don't want to see you again."

"What did you say?"

"For all I know, you could be making this whole thing up. How do I know you even talked to Thelma Lee? You didn't trust me; I don't trust you. Our business is over. I'd like you to leave."

"You throwing me out?"

"Yes, I'm throwing you out."

I didn't realize my legs were shaking until I tried to stand up, but I forced myself to stand straight, move toward the door. He stood up and followed me but stopped when I opened it.

"I'm asking you to leave now, sir," I said, my voice trembling.

"You sure about that?" he said, his voice cagey, cute, like he was flirting with me.

I nodded, too scared to trust my voice again. He looked me up and down, sizing me up, then walked out the door. But he stopped at the top of the stairs and stood to the side. Sweet Thing and Jimson

Weed were coming up, slow and with concerted effort. When Jimson Weed saw him, he stepped back against the wall. Treyman Barnes looked at him hard, his eyes narrowed into mean slits.

"Where I know you from, man?" he said.

"Hell," Jimson Weed muttered, so low I barely heard him. He roughly pushed Sweet Thing into my office in front of him. I stood back amazed as the two of them barged in. They looked like extras from a movie circa 1960. He sported a forest green polyester suit, flared pants, Nehru jacket, and a white turtleneck that fit tight around his thick neck. He was built like a fighter, and the suit complemented his physique. He obviously hadn't gained a pound since he'd bought it forty years ago.

She was dressed grandly—from the decade before: crisp seersucker suit, neat white gloves, small black hat with a veil that reeked of mothballs, which I smelled as she'd whisked past. In one hand, she held a black plastic handbag fastened with a fake diamond clasp, and in the other, a pink and white umbrella, meant, I assumed, to block the sun. When she sat down, he stood behind her like a soldier-protector—hands at side, back ramrod-stiff. She preened like a reigning monarch for a moment, then opened her handbag, took out my card, and placed it on my desk.

"You told me to come if I needed something, so here I am," she said.

"You still working for him?" Jimson Weed nodded toward the door where "the Devil," as he'd called him before, had just exited.

"No. I'm not working for Mr. Barnes anymore," I said wearily.

"He in that big building over there on Broad Street, the one they been working on, ain't he? He rich now, ain't he? He paid for that fancy car he got parked outside with blood, you know that?"

I didn't give him an answer; I doubted if he was looking for one.

"If he came for that child, ain't no way in hell he's going to get her back," said Jimson Weed. "And if he try, Sweet Thing got something in that bag for folks who mess with her family. I taught her to use it, too. She can aim straight, and she can aim sure."

I glanced down at Sweet Thing's handbag and realized he was talking about a gun. Older women who grew up in the South often kept their .22s next to their compacts and combs in their fancy handbags. My aunt Odessa, a strong, beautiful woman as tough as nails, *never* left the house without "protection," and she wasn't talking condoms. Sweet Thing was of the same generation, so she was probably packing, too. All the more reason to get these two out of my office . . . and out of my life.

"Do you know where the baby is?" I asked.

They shook their heads in unison, as if they were attached by a string.

"Last we saw her she was with Thelma Lee," said Sweet Thing. She shifted her eyes to Jimson, then glanced down at her hands. He stood mum, good soldier that he was.

I sat for a moment, taking them both in, wondering how much they really knew about anything.

"What can I do for you today?" I said, praying this would be the last time I said those words today.

"We come about our niece, Thelma Lee. She's disappeared, and we don't know what's happened to her," said Sweet Thing. "We want you to find our niece for us. I want us all to be a family again—me, Jimson, Thelma Lee, and that baby."

"The baby doesn't belong to you," I said firmly, but not without sympathy for these poor souls, as lost in yesterday's lives as they were in its clothes. I wondered if they knew about the death of the other niece yet, the one Sweet Thing called Lily. Was it my place to tell them? Best to leave it to the cops. "It's very important that you talk to the police about Thelma Lee's disappearance. There have been some other . . . developments that you should know about as soon as possible." The police must know Lilah's next of kin by now, and when they asked about Thelma Lee, Lilah was bound to come up. Let the cops break the bad news. They knew how to do it better than me, and they got paid for it.

"I called them this morning when she didn't come home last night, but they said she was a runaway before and they wouldn't look for her. She hadn't been gone a day, so that's why we came to you," said Sweet Thing.

"She's only been gone a day?"

"She came home late on Tuesday. She was real scared like, and—"

"And what?" I asked.

Sweet Thing took a deep breath. "I think somebody tried to hurt her. She had blood on her clothes. She came in and . . . and dropped something off . . . then left real quick. Said she'd call me later, but then she didn't come back."

"What did she drop off?"

Sweet Thing glanced at Jimson Weed, who shrugged.

"Did you tell the cops about the blood?" I said, trying a different direction.

She nodded that she had. "Maybe you should call them again. There might be some new . . . information. Please. Call them again."

"All they'll say was she's a runaway, and that's all she is to them," Sweet Thing said.

"How many times has she run away?"

"That girl ain't no good. She don't cause you nothing but grief, Sweet Thing. Take what she give you and enjoy it. It's a good thing she's gone."

"Don't say that, Jimson," she said, the first time she'd raised her voice at him since I'd seen them together.

"I'm sorry, baby." He brought her fingers to his lips and kissed them. I glanced away, embarrassed. "She ain't interested in looking for the girl. Let's be on our way, baby. Let's just be on our way."

"Okay, my sweet Jimson," she said, her voice soft and broken.

You ever have a man love you like that?

What would that *really* feel like, I wondered.

Sweet Thing went out first, head bowed low. He opened the door, following behind her. Before he closed it, he turned around for one last look at me, then spit right in the center of my newly cleaned rug.

"For devilish ways," he said as he slammed the door behind him.

I sat there for a moment too shocked to move. What could have made him do it? I wondered. I'd seen my grandma do it once, spit sideways at somebody, but never on somebody's floor. It was what people did to rid themselves of evil, she said, to get it out of your mouth. What was he trying to get out of his mouth? Or was it me he was spitting at? Maybe he was just losing his mind, and I should leave it at that. I looked at that spit for a minute, nasty as it was on my office floor, not sure what to do next. Then I started to laugh.

They say tears and laughter come from about the same place, and sometimes it's just a matter of chance what comes out first. It was laughter for me today, and I laughed until my sides ached. I laughed at that fool of a man and what he had just done, and Treyman Barnes and his silly ass self, and the look on DeWayne's face when I threw that glass against the wall. Then I started feeling "devilish" (like Jimson Weed might say) and laughed about the way DeWayne's latest wife had left him high and dry, and about how all of those damn people—Lilah Love, Jimson Weed, Treyman Barnes—were finally out of my life. I started thinking about Jamal then, and I felt tears coming, but I wasn't ready to cry yet, not until this whole thing was good and over. So I got up, smudged that man's spit into the carpet with the toe of my shoe, and headed downstairs to Wyvetta Green's to see what she could do for me.

NINE

WYVETTA GREEN BENT OVER an elderly client, tenderly arranging her sunset red curls into thin ringlets. The client, Miss Peterson, was roughly the same age as Sweet Thing and wore a hot pink jumpsuit and a thick gold chain around her long, birdlike neck. She was a tiny woman who was further dwarfed by Wyvetta's lush pink chair.

"There you go, Miss Peterson. This color really suits you," Wyvetta said, giving her a motherly pat as she glanced over her shoulder at me. "Hey, girl, how you doing?"

"I've seen better days."

"Wasn't that you up there doing all that laughing?"

"You could hear me down here?"

"I hear a lot of stuff you don't think I can," Wyvetta said with a chuckle.

"Some days you gotta laugh to keep from crying," Miss Peterson chimed in.

Wyvetta shook her head. "I seen some strange ones climbing those stairs to your office, honey, but this morning just about took the cake."

All I could do was roll my eyes.

"Wyvetta, was that Treyman Barnes parked outside the Biscuit just now?" Miss Peterson asked.

"Yes, I believe it was."

"What's he doing in this neighborhood?"

Wyvetta shrugged, throwing me a covert glance.

"I knew his daddy," Miss Peterson continued. "We called him Trey. Knew him *good,* too. Inside *and* out. Didn't you tell me once you knew the son? Maybe he was over here to see you?" She added a sly wink.

"I knew his son, but not like you knew his daddy, Miss Peterson," Wyvetta corrected her.

"You're an inspiration, Wyvetta. I just wish I'd known you when I had more hair." Miss Peterson, taking the hint, changed the subject.

"You look just fine with the hair you have, Miss Peterson. Why don't you settle down in that chair across the room and Maydell will do something with them nails? How about a pedicure?"

"Ooh, I like that! Today I feel like treating myself like the treasure I am!" Maydell, seated in a rolling chair across the room, dragged the cart of lotions and polishes to where Miss Peterson sat. A recent hire, Maydell was a plump, light-skinned woman in her mid twenties with blond dreadlocks and bright red lipstick. She was dressed in a cerise and pink smock, which matched the color scheme of the shop. She had a charming, lazy smile that made you like her, but her slowness in other departments got on Wyvetta's nerves, who threatened to fire her "do-nothing behind" at least once a week. But Maydell was good with customers, and they were generous with tips, so it all worked out.

Wyvetta studied my face. "You down here for them brows?"

"The works, Wyvetta. I need the works."

She nodded as if she understood, then whispered, "You know I got that you-know-what stashed in the back room if you want to grab yourself a nip."

I shook my head. If I got started on that bourbon, no telling when I'd stop.

"Well, you're in luck today, sweetie. I just had a cancellation. Come on in here and sit down. I'll be with you in a New York minute."

I settled down in one of her cushiony chairs, and she fastened a cerise smock around my neck.

"You gonna have some color today, Miss Tamara? Everyone loves that Sunset Red!" said Maydell from her perch at Miss Peterson's fingertips.

"Not today, Maydell." I leaned back in my chair, closed my eyes, and let Wvyetta's magical fingers go to work on my scalp.

I thought about my son. There had been such fear in his eyes when I'd left him this morning, and I'd never seen that before. *Goodbye, Jamal, I'll see you soon,* I'd told him, but we both knew there was no truth in that. There was no telling when I'd see him again. Too many things—cops, Lilah's murder, her killer—stood in the way.

She got real mad, and she kept arguing with whoever it was and said it was nobody's business what she did with what was hers.

So what was hers? Baby Dal, of course.

Stolen property, you might say.

Lilah Love had left home and come back in town, and more than likely had been killed because of it. I just had to figure out why.

"Miss Peterson, you used to go out with Mr. Barnes. I used to go out with his grandson, Troy. We didn't have a lot in common, but we got real serious, for a while. He was always sweet and polite. My mama was mad as a hornet when I broke up with him." Maydell's high-pitched voice brought me into the present.

Miss Peterson sucked her teeth. "Is he a hoodlum like his granddaddy was? The fruit don't fall far from the tree."

"Nooo, Troy ain't no gangster, Miss Peterson. He's a hero. That's what I call him anyway. He joined the army to fight for his country. He's a true-blue hero. Was his granddaddy a hoodlum?"

"Yes, he was."

"You used to go out with gangstas, Miss Peterson?" Maydell didn't hide her curiosity bordering on admiration.

"Ain't nothing good about going out with a gangster, Maydell," said Miss Peterson. "But I was wild when I was young, and Treyman Barnes was the wildest hoodlum in town. Boy was so light-skinned, folks thought he was white. Had the white folks fooled, too, 'cause they let him run the rackets in all them fancy clubs used to serve the colored."

"Fancy clubs in Newark? You putting me on, Miss Peterson."

"Fancy as some of them over there in Atlantic City. Why there was the Kinney over there on August and Arlington, that place on Boston Street. There was the Key Club and half a dozen other spots where folks—hustlers, gangsters, anybody with good money looking for a good time—could hang out. And the hoodlums dressed as clean as your mama's mouth. You didn't see nobody's trousers dropped down around their drawers like you do nowadays. Trey Barnes was the cleanest of the clean."

Her words brought back the tales my grandmother used to tell of a Newark long gone. This had once been a town of fun and folly that people had been proud to call their home. But all that was left were memories, and they'd soon be as dead as the gardenias the women once pinned in their hair.

"Kids shooting each other up over nothing—this town wasn't always like that. This town had class, even the robbers and thugs."

"Even the robbers and thugs? That's something, Miss Peterson. Things sure have changed."

"Yes, they have, Maydell, and not for the better. Wyvetta, where you know Treyman Barnes from?" She glanced back at Wyvetta.

"School," Wyvetta said, rinsing my hair with warm water.

"You think Troy's daddy, Mr. Barnes, is a gangster like his granddaddy was?" asked Maydell.

Wyvetta eased my head off the sink, and as she wrapped it with a towel, she threw Maydell a look that made the girl drop her eyes and put down her polish. But a look wasn't enough to stop Miss Peterson.

"You know, Wyvetta, they say he's tied up in the rackets, too, and he was mixed up in that mess that went on over there on Avon Avenue a while back. They say there wasn't a trace of nothing on his hands, 'cept blood. Five good men died that day, and one of 'em went to my church. You think Treyman Barnes was mixed up in that mess?"

I felt Wyvetta's hands tense as she toweled my hair, and her voice dropped an octave when she spoke. "I don't know nothing about no mess on Avon Avenue, and I don't know nothing about where Treyman Barnes sticks his hands, and if I were you, Miss Peterson, I'd keep my thoughts about Treyman Barnes and Avon Avenue to myself," she said.

"Ooooh!" squealed Maydell.

"Hush your mouth, girl," said Wyvetta. "Time for you to go under the dryer," she said to me, and promptly guided me to the bank of pink hair dryers at the far end of the room and turned the dryer on high, effectively blocking any more eavesdropping.

Wyvetta must have thought my ears needed protecting from whatever it was Miss Peterson might have had to say, but I wasn't so sure. The more I knew about the man, the better off I'd be. The evil look he'd given me had sent a chill up my spine, and despite the heat of the dryer on my neck, I could still feel it.

But Barnes was much too smart to murder Lilah. Yet murderers, particularly very powerful ones, rarely thought about consequences until it was too late. Men like that considered themselves above the law. But what would he gain? Maybe she had something on him that he couldn't afford to have get out. Or on someone he loved. His wife? His son? He wasn't strong enough to kill her himself, so he would have had somebody do it for him. Somebody strong with a grudge against Lilah. But then that person would have something on him, too. Unless he, or she, had as much to lose as Barnes. Or as much to gain. Who could that be? Turk? Barnes's son? The cops might even think it was me, particularly if they could connect us through our Jamaica days. And if they connected her to me, they could connect her to my son.

By the time my hair was dry, Miss Peterson had left, and Maydell had wheeled her chair and cart in position to do my nails. She broke out something called Vixen Red, and when the polish was dry on my finger- and toenails, I felt right vixenish. Wvyetta did my brows like she'd promised, and I had to admit, it made a big difference.

"Once a month," she said, as she picked off the last piece of wax, then soothed my skin with cream that smelled like strawberries. She wouldn't take any money for my brows, said it was a favor between friends, and I didn't fight her on it. My three hours in the Biscuit had cost me as much as a silk blouse from Bendel's. But it was money well spent; I felt like a new woman when I walked out of the salon.

It was raining by then, a fine, prickly drizzle too light for an umbrella but good on my skin. I turned my head up and breathed in the air. It smelled fresh and clean, and suddenly I knew that everything just might turn out all right. It had to. I hadn't gone a dozen steps when I heard his voice.

"Tamara."

I turned to face him. "Basil, why are you here?"

"You, of course," he said, with that dazzling smile that breaks me down. "Rain becomes you."

"Where did you get that line?" I asked, and smiled despite myself.

"Pretty corny, huh?"

"Not your style, Basil."

"You bring out the foolish boy in me."

"Oh, go away!" I said, and almost meant it.

He glanced at his watch. "Time for a drink before you go home?"

"How do you know that's where I'm going?"

"Wild guess. For old times? Come." He grabbed my hand, and, as it always did, his touch went straight down my spine, but I pulled away.

"I don't think so, Basil. You know where our drinks usually end up."

He smiled then, and I returned it. There was no lying about that. Maybe it was the memory of those old times or that smile, or that I realized perhaps this was the best way to say goodbye. Or simply because I didn't want all that money I'd just spent on looking good going back to an empty house and a sink of dirty dishes, so I said I would come.

A new bar called Illusions had opened up down the street from Wyvetta's salon, and we headed to it. I remembered the place when it was called The Rainbow's Inn, a tacky little dive with a bad color scheme, and some of the old décor remained. Each stool was a different color, and the ceiling was filled with multicolored rainbows arching nowhere. But they'd added new subdued lighting and tables in the back, and as we walked toward them, I remembered all the times we'd been together: that first kiss, so innocently given, which had rocked my joke of a marriage to DeWayne; the mountains in Jamaica when I thought he was dead; and the night in Atlantic City when he'd wept about his daughter's death. I wondered if he remembered those times, too, and what he was feeling.

But this was goodbye, I reminded myself. I had a man now, and I didn't want to blow it. We didn't speak as we sat down at a small table in the back. Our knees touched, and I pulled away. I'd remembered how carefully I'd avoided DeWayne Curtis's leg under his kitchen table. Seemed like I was always trying to pull away from the touch of some man's knee these days. But it was definitely not revulsion this time.

"May I help you?" A honey brown sister with fake green eyes and too much cleavage sauntered to our table, her emerald eyes locked squarely on Basil.

"Wine, please. Red."

"Ain't got no red wine. We got bourbon, scotch, gin. Stuff folks usually get in a bar."

"Diet Coke, do you have that?" She took her eyes off Basil long enough to throw me a nasty glance.

"And for the gentleman?"

"Red Stripe, please," Basil said with his usual smile, which she coyly returned.

No tip for this hussy, I said to myself.

When she'd left, he said, "Let's go somewhere else. There's a better place not too far from here, and you can get whatever you want. Champagne, good rum—"

"I'll stick with the Coke." Alcohol would loosen my tongue, to say nothing of everything else. The waitress brought our drinks, and I took a sip of mine, which was as weak as water.

"Fate is having its way with us these days. First Monday and now today. Although I had a hand in things today. I wanted to see you again. But surely you know my feelings by now."

I nodded before I thought better of it. I did know much about him but really knew nothing at all.

Or was I fooling myself?

"Why were you there Monday, in Treyman Barnes's building?" I asked, trying to turn the conversation away from my—and his— feelings.

"How do you know I was there to see him?" His eyes read mine as quickly as I read those of other people.

"Were you?"

"No."

"Don't lie to me."

"Business. Ask me no more," he said, with a finality that told me I'd get nothing more from him. There were things about Basil I didn't understand, hidden places he went, secrets he told no one. Sometimes I guessed them, but most I didn't want to know. And that added to his mystery, and as dangerous as I knew he was, it made him irresistible.

"I promise, it had nothing to do with you." He sensed my next question.

"Promise?"

"Promise."

"Then what did he want?"

"I turned him down, so it doesn't matter."

"Are you telling me the truth?"

"I don't lie to you . . . about important things," he said, shifting his eyes from mine, a sure sign he did.

And I had had my fill of lying men. I rose to leave, and he stood up with me, gently pulled me back down. His touch, as always, went places it had no business going.

"I turned his offer down. I can't tell you more."

"Did it have something to do with a woman named Lilah Love?"

"No," he said firmly, but I didn't know what he was thinking. "Were you there to see him?"

"I was working for him," I said.

He glanced at me, and I couldn't read what was in his eyes. He picked up his drink, took a sip, put it down.

"He's not someone you toy with, Tamara," he said. "He was once, and still can be, a very dangerous man."

"They say that about you."

He chuckled, amused. "Not to you. What were you doing for him?"

"Business. He pays good."

"So you need money?" I was touched by the concern in his tone and in his gaze. He'd helped me out more times than I could remember, usually anonymously, but I always knew where the money came from. Only Jake knew more about my often precarious finances.

I shook my head. "For once, I'm fine."

"And your son. How is your boy?"

I couldn't speak; my feelings must have shown on my face.

"Tell me."

"He's with his father."

"Does this have anything to do with Barnes?"

I didn't answer because I didn't know, and that was on my face, too.

Basil Dupre *was* a dangerous man, but he was a kind one, too, and because he knew intimately a world that I only occasionally entered, I knew he would try to protect me in ways only he knew how. He took my hand, and I felt his strength in that gesture.

"You know anything you need I will do. Anything." I smiled slightly because I knew it was true, but I couldn't trust my voice to speak.

He kissed me on the cheek and stood up. "I'll be leaving town in a day or two. May I call you before I leave?"

I nodded that he could, and he walked out, dropping fifty bucks on the bar for the waitress. After he'd gone, I realized Larry Walton hadn't even entered my mind.

TEN

AVOIDED THE PITYING STARE of the green-eyed waitress on my way out of the bar. She probably wondered what in the hell was wrong with me letting a man like that out of my sight. I wondered what in the hell was wrong with me, too. Then I reminded myself—there was no future in it, so I let it go. I thought about dropping back by the Biscuit. I could use that shot of bourbon Wyvetta had mentioned just about now. But the shop was full, and Wyvetta was grinning, styling, and in her glory. No time for me and my burdens. There was nowhere else to go but my office, so I trudged upstairs, locked my office door to ward off uninvited guests, and gazed at the dancing fish on my computer screen for the next ten minutes.

I finally called Jamal. He sounded tired and depressed, and that worried me. I knew he was going through hell and that DeWayne didn't have the good sense to help him get through it. My ex-husband was about as introspective as a glass of milk—a man who hopped from one crisis to the next as carelessly as he did women's beds. Jamal needed help. A good friend had died and a woman he befriended (he would call it that anyway) had been brutally murdered. Add cops to that dish, and the meal was poisoned. Jamal needed wisdom and sympathy, while DeWayne, the perpetual adolescent, was only capable of throwing money at him, which he did with abandon.

In breathless wonder, Jamal told me that they were going to dinner every night and had ordered wrestling matches from pay TV. They had tickets to three fights in Atlantic City on Saturday and Sunday night, and DeWayne had promised to teach him to drive. *That's great, Son. That's great, Son. That's great, Son.* I repeated like a mantra, but I was worried and wanted him back home.

So I sat at my desk, listening to cars honking and teenagers screaming until I couldn't stand it anymore. At least, my neighborhood was quieter than my office, though nothing like DeWayne's, with its cookie-cutter houses with their neat green lawns. I wondered which one of his wives had cosigned the mortgage for that place. Part of a settlement, no doubt. DeWayne was the kind of man who would gladly take alimony from a woman, and that house, cute and cozy as it was, had probably been part of some deal. Anything to get the fool out of her life. But it was his now, and the prices in his neighborhood were soaring. Unlike mine, where prices dropped every time somebody got mugged. It was my parents' home, and I loved it for that, but I couldn't help wishing they'd made their lifetime investment in a different place, like Sweet Thing's neighborhood in Jersey City. I'd be sitting pretty now if they had.

I thought again about Jimson Weed spitting on my floor and got mad all over again. I called Larry to take my mind off spit and worrying about my son, but he was so full of chatter about the position he was running for, and how much money he would make and other things I didn't give a damn about, that my mind strayed back to Basil Dupre, and the look in his eyes when he kissed me goodbye.

"Then we're still on for tomorrow?" Larry asked.

"Huh?" I'd hardly heard him.

"Tomorrow night. I'm coming over tomorrow for dinner, remember? Have you forgotten?" His impatience annoyed me.

"Of course not. Tomorrow night."

"So how's Jamal doing with summer school?"

"Jamal's away."

Pause.

"Away?"

I didn't want to hear it, about how the way I make my living had endangered my son or how he'd be better off with his father or how a boy needs a man, so I lied.

"DeWayne wanted to take him to a couple of fights in Atlantic City, so he's staying down there for a couple of days."

"Lucky kid."

"Yeah."

"Good for him, good for us."

"Yeah."

"Tomorrow, then. Love you."

Why hadn't I just told the man what was really going on?

I paid a few bills online and then went to MySpace to see if Jamal had posted anything new. I was relieved to see he hadn't. I wrote a few letters, dropped them in the mailbox on the way out the door, then stopped by my favorite takeout spot for some fried whiting and coleslaw. It was close to ten when I pulled into my driveway.

The house was dark, and I cursed out loud. It was bad enough coming home to an empty house without walking into darkness. My hunger, sharpened by the smell of fried fish, finally propelled me out of the car and into my kitchen. I snapped on the switch, cursing when the light didn't come on. I'd left it on when I pulled out with nothing on my mind but Jamal, so it must have burned out. The hall light was out, too. I put the fish on top of the stove and went to get a flashlight and spare bulbs from the linen closet at the top of the stairs.

I heard the sound when I was halfway up, and I stopped dead, stood still, listened. Footsteps now, scampering across the hall into Jamal's room. Was it him? Of course not. I'd just talked to him at De-Wayne's. Somebody looking for him? My heart beat fast; sweat popped out on the back of my neck.

Footsteps again, but bold this time, like he didn't give a damn, like he wasn't afraid, and that scared me more than anything else. Was he looking for Jamal or something in his room? Had he searched the others before I came? How long had he been here?

I backed down the stairs, one step at a time. Where was the phone? I'd left it in Jamal's room when I'd called his friends the night before. My gun was upstairs, too, in the safe in my bedroom; there was no getting to it now, and I'd be damned if I went up these stairs with nothing in my hands but sweat.

Whoever killed Lilah Love is here.

The fear that came with that thought settled in the pit of my stomach, so deep I could hardly breathe. How had he gotten in? I saw no sign of the back door being forced. The basement door? Had I locked it? No. Had I even bothered with the top latch on the front door? I'd been in such a rush to get out, I wasn't sure what I'd locked and what I hadn't, and I left without setting the alarm. Damn thing didn't work half the time anyway, but I should have turned it on. One more mistake.

The roof from my window is low, and it's not that far from the ground.

Jamal's window must still be open. If he jumped down, then somebody could climb up. Somebody with arms as big as my thighs, strong enough to pull himself up, strong enough to wham a fist through a woman's throat.

Damn it!

Which one was nearer, the back or the front door? About the same distance. I'd go out the front. Closer to the street, easier to get somebody's attention. I took one stair at a time backward, cursing the one that always creaked.

Stopping again, I listened, then turned around heading for the front door. Somebody moved. Feet scampering across the floor, like a kid playing hide-and-seek. Were the steps heading to the stairs? Trying to get to me before I got out? The light went on in Jamal's bedroom, throwing everything into shadow. I stumbled downstairs toward the living room, heading for the door. It was then that she called out.

"Miss Hayle, is that you? If you got a gun, please don't shoot me, Miss Hayle. And if it ain't Miss Hayle, I got a knife *and* a gun, and I know how to use them. Is that you, Miss Hayle?"

I'd recognize that scared, shaky little voice anywhere.

"Thelma Lee. What in the hell are you doing in my house?"

She ran downstairs, two steps at a time like Jamal, stopping halfway down.

"It's Trinity. Please call me Trinity. I don't like *Thelma Lee*. Please don't shoot me. I'm up here 'cause it was dark down there and I was scared. Please don't shoot me."

"Do you have any weapons?" I tried to keep my voice from shaking.

"Naw, I was lying."

Lying now or then?

"I want you to step into the hall with your hands high above your head so I can see them. Do you understand me? I *do* have a weapon, a gun."

I drew back in the shadows, listening to every move she made as she came down the stairs. If she had a gun instead of a knife, I could duck into the basement and get out fast through the door. If not, there was no reason to be scared; she was nothing but a kid. I could handle a knife.

I moved behind the banister so I'd be behind her to make sure her hands were over her head. She came down slowly and stood in front of me, hands held high, standing so close I had to take a step back.

I was expecting a younger version of Lilah Love, a spitfire of a girl-woman who would turn a man's head before he knew it was turned, but baby sister was nothing like Lilah, with her lime-colored silk and tacky gold jewelry. She was dressed all in black like her *Matrix* namesake—without the curves or style—tight jeans, tighter T-shirt, sneakers, black leather jacket (as hot as it was!). I wondered if she knew Trinity's moves, the karate kicks and lethal chops. She wore a gold bracelet with bells on it that jingled when she moved and re-minded me of Lilah's anklet. She was built "thick," as the kids like to say, heavier than me by about twenty pounds. Baby fat, I figured, not seasoned muscle, but I couldn't be sure. She moved slowly, like an old woman just starting her day or a toddler waking up from her after-noon nap.

"Take four steps forward," I said, still standing behind her. My eyes had adjusted to the darkened room, and I didn't see any weapon.

"Can I put my arms down, Miss Hayle? I'm getting tired."

"No, keep them up." I had to be sure about the knife. I quickly frisked her, then told her to relax but to stay where she was. I turned on a lamp in the living room so I could see her face clearly. Sweet Thing was all over the girl: high cheekbones, sharp like a Sioux, dark red-brown Indian skin, straight black hair pulled tight against her scalp and fastened with a black and gold scrunchy.

She began to sob, covering her face with her fingers, which were thick as a man's and topped with broken black nails.

I gave her a minute, then asked, "You okay?"

"No!"

"I'm going to ask you this again before I call the cops. What are you doing in my house?"

Her words came tumbling out high and fast like they had when we'd talked on the phone Monday night. "Please don't call the police, Miss Hayle. Please don't call them. I was scared, that's why I came here. I was scared, real scared. I saw something on Tuesday night I never want to see again in my whole life! I don't want the person who did it coming after me. I know he's coming after me next 'cause I was with him. I don't want—"

"You've been here since last night?" I asked in disbelief.

"I had nowhere to go," she answered in a small voice. "It happened last night, and after it happened, I went to my aunt's and took Baby Dal, then I came here because I was scared."

"Wait a minute. So where's the baby now?"

"At Aunt Edna's."

I thought again about my conversation with Sweet Thing and Jimson Weed earlier today. Neither had bothered to mention that the "something" the girl had dropped off was a baby.

"So you saw them last night?"

"I saw my Aunt Edna, gave her the baby, then left." She started sobbing again. I put my hand on her shoulder.

"Calm down!" I said, and sat down beside her.

"I *can't* calm down! Not after what I saw last night. I been crying all night about Turk. I can't calm down!"

"Turk! What do you know about Turk? Isn't that Lilah's boyfriend?"

She started to cry again, and her voice cracked with hoarseness when she spoke. "My sister is dead, Miss Hayle. My big sister is dead. Lily is dead, and I don't know what I'm going to do about it. I loved Lily. She didn't love me, but I loved her. More than anything, I loved her. She was my mama's baby just like me."

"Lily? You're talking about Lilah Love?" What was it with these people and names? I wondered. Some profound dissatisfaction with who they were, I figured.

"Lily. Please call her Lily! She started calling herself Lilah when she left home, then she married this guy named Sammy Lee Love, and she said never to mention the name *Sweets* again. *Love* suited her better. That really hurt my aunt's feelings, but Lily didn't care. So she took his name just because she liked the way it sounded, then he got killed somewhere, and—"

"I know the rest." I studied the girl for a minute or two, then said,

"Do you know who killed your sister?" She looked at me strangely, her eyes big and questioning.

"No."

"Do you know who the cops think killed her?"

She shook her head. "No."

"They think it was Turk Orlando."

She looked alarmed. "Why do they think that?"

"The evidence they have points to it."

"What evidence?"

"Does it bother you that you were fooling around with the man who killed your sister?" I said, ignoring her question.

She got serious for a minute, then narrowed her eyes. "If I thought he killed my sister, I'd have to kill him back. I would have had to kill him back instead of letting the person who killed him do it. I would have—"

"Are you telling me Turk Orlando is dead?"

"And nobody knows it but me," she wailed. "I'm scared the person that done it will be coming after me next. Just because of that baby. I know it's because of that baby. Me and Turk didn't mean no harm. We—"

I stood up, ready to call the police and tell them what the girl had just said, but she grabbed my arm, the bells on her gold bracelet jingling, her grip on my arm stronger than I expected. I thought about how deeply Lilah's nails had dug into my wrist, and I wondered, for an instant, if I'd misread the girl, yet I didn't have a sense of danger, and my instincts are usually good about that kind of thing, so I sat back down.

"Please don't call the police. I know that's what you were going to do. If you call the police, I'm gone and I'll end up dead. There ain't no way they can protect me. I know that. They don't care nothing about nobody who looks like me anyway."

I thought about what Sweet Thing had told me about telling the cops. That was probably the only truthful thing she had said. Black girls gone missing were never given more than short shrift by the police. A few days ago, I'd seen a story about a fifteen-year-old Newark girl who had disappeared for damn near two weeks. It was tucked into the back pages of the paper, right under an ad for real estate. No headlines, no quotes, nothing but ten skimpy lines. If the girl had been white and the town had been Short Hills, it would have made the six o'clock news the day she'd gone. Truth be told, the only people who gave a damn about black women were other black women.

But if Thelma had witnessed a murder like she said, especially if the victim was Turk, then they'd want to know what she'd seen. But if Turk was dead, then who had murdered Lilah Love? I glanced at her hands again. They were big enough to go through somebody's throat, somebody as small as Lilah. But she wouldn't murder her own sister.

"I'm tired of sitting here in the dark. There are some lightbulbs in the closet upstairs. I'm going to go up and get them. When I come back, I want to know everything that happened, you understand me?"

She nodded that she did, and I went upstairs for the lightbulbs, stopping in my room for my .38, which I strapped in an ankle band holster under my pants leg. She was still sitting on the stairs, head hung low, when I came back down. I screwed in the bulbs, then put the kettle on for some tea. She came into the kitchen and sat down at the table.

"My Aunt Edna used to have a table like this when I was a little girl," she said. "When my mama would come home Sunday mornings, we'd sit and have tea and cookies, just like real little ladies, my mama used to say. Just like real little ladies."

She ran her hand across the table's surface as if stroking a cat and closed her eyes as if remembering. It was a nice piece of furniture, I had to agree with her on that. It was oak and heavy, better suited perhaps to a fancy dining room than my dowdy kitchen, but it gave my space an elegance that it badly needed. I'd bought it the year I left De-Wayne Curtis, my first purchase without him, my celebration of independence. Jamal had been a little boy then, and the salesman told me he'd be a grandfather with grandchildren before it wore out. It was a splendid old table that I could easily imagine in Sweet Thing's grand old house.

"I've had this table a long time, probably longer than you've been alive," I said, and she grinned. She had a pretty smile, with gapped teeth that gave her an elfin look.

"That's like my aunt's old house. She says old things have memories, and you should never sell them."

"I think she's right. Are you hungry?" My fish sandwich was cold, so I put it in the refrigerator; there wasn't enough for two anyway.

"I went out this morning and got some chocolate donuts from that Dunkin' Donuts down the street, and I had McDonald's Tuesday night before . . . well, before you know what. I had two burgers, and Turk had a Big Mac. That Big Mac was Turk's last meal. Do you think that's right, that a Big Mac should be a man's last meal on earth?"

I glanced at the girl and shook my head. "Honey, I don't know," I said, but I was struck by the fact that she'd gone out for Dunkin'

Donuts the morning after seeing a man brutally murdered. What was really going on with her?

"He must have liked them because he was always eating them."

"Well, I guess that must have been his favorite meal, and a man should have his favorite meal before he dies," I said, not sure what else to say. She nodded, then wiped the tears off her face with her hand. I gave her a napkin, and she blew her nose.

I made some tuna fish sandwiches, light on the mayonnaise, and brewed some tea. She gobbled down two sandwiches, loaded her tea with four teaspoons of sugar, slurped it down, and burped.

"So where is Turk now?" I asked when she was finished. "His body, I mean."

"I left him over there, in that old motel off the turnpike." I sipped my tea without comment. That rathole of a place had been a notorious spot for live-in whores, thieves, and general lowlifes for the last twenty-five years. I knew of at least four unsolved murders that had been committed there. That must have been the "shit hole" where Treyman Barnes said she'd told him to meet her with the baby. But I wasn't ready to mention Barnes yet or anything she'd supposedly told him. I wanted to see how well their stories meshed.

"Why did you and Turk go there?" I kept any hint of judgment out of my voice.

"That's where my mama died, and I always go there to be with her spirit."

"When did she die?"

"When I was a baby. Somebody put a knife straight through her heart. Right through it."

Her words sent a chill through me, but I tried not to show it.

"How do you know she died there?"

"I found the police report in my Aunt Edna's room a couple of years back, so I know the exact place. Room 311. That's the exact room. They ain't hardly even changed anything about the room. And I'm happy about that. That room is a secret I keep with my mama, and she ain't telling nobody. And don't you tell nobody either. Hardly anybody knows I go there, except Aunt Edna, the lady at my school, and a couple of the guys who work there. They're real nice."

"And your aunt doesn't object?"

"The lady at school, my guidance counselor, told my aunt not to let me go there no more. She said it didn't do me no good, that it might end up making me crazy, but that was a while ago. I told my aunt it would make me crazy if I didn't go there, and she said it was okay, if it made me feel closer to my mama. That's the only place I go when I'm not home."

"Do you go back to that room often?"

"Sometimes, if nobody's in it. I feel like they should make it a shrine or something, even though my mama died a long time ago, but I guess they won't. Maybe I will someday—get rich enough to buy that nasty old place, burn it down, and turn it into a garden for my mama, and fill it with roses and pink flowers."

"If somebody's there, where do you go?"

"The same room on another floor—211 or 411. Sometimes I just sit in the lobby. They don't say nothing to me. They don't care much. Men try to pick me up, but I know what I am, and I'm not that."

I felt my eyes well with tears, so I got up to put more water in the kettle so she wouldn't see them. I knew now what her mama had been, how she probably died, and what that had done to this child. I spent more time than I needed running water and filling the kettle.

"Do you think the spirits of killed people stay where they die?"

"I don't know, honey. The dead have their secrets same as the living."

"If they do, then Turk must be right up there with Mama, in that same room. But I hope he's not. I don't think she'd like him much."

"I don't think she'd like him much either," I said, and sat down across from her. "So your aunt brought you up?"

"Aunt Edna raised me up when Mama got killed. She was Mama's big sister. Aunt Edna raised Mama up, too, when they came up from Mississippi."

"How old was your mama?" Aunt Sweet Thing must be younger than I thought.

"Mama was in her thirties when she died. Aunt Edna was twenty years older."

"How old is your aunt now?" I've never been good at math, especially doing it in my head; I have trouble making change at the corner store. Thelma must have noticed my confusion.

"Seventy-something. She was fifty-eight when my mama died. I was just a little baby. Lily was twelve. Lily got Mama's name. At least she could carry that around with her. But then she went and changed it to *Lilah*, like she changed *Sweets* to *Love* because it was prettier, but I don't think there's nothing prettier than your mama's name. Mama called me Thelma Lee, after her mama. Thelma Lee Sweets."

I thought back to my first visit with Sweet Thing and Jimson

Weed. The dead Lily they'd mentioned had been Thelma Lee's mother. Sweet Thing's baby sister.

"And Jimson Weed? How does he come into this?"

Thelma Lee's face darkened. "He started hanging around Aunt Edna right after my mama died, at least that's what Lily said. She said he was like some old vulture hanging around my aunt. Trying to pick her clean."

"Sounds like you don't like him too much."

"He acts like he owns my Aunt Edna or something, that she belongs to his crazy behind. That's why Lily left four years after Mama died, because of the way he treated Aunt Edna. Like he's the only one who cares about what happens to her."

She drank what was left in her cup, and I asked if she wanted some more. She nodded, and I put the kettle back on. Neither of us spoke until it whistled and I'd fixed her another cup. She sipped it slowly, gaze fastened on the cup. After she finished drinking, she placed it back on the table, carefully, as if it took everything she had to put it down. She shook her bracelet and smiled.

"Did your aunt give you this?" I asked.

"My aunt gave it to me when I turned twelve. It used to belong to my mama. She had two. Aunt Edna gave one to Lily, too, right after Mama died, then she gave one to me. It's supposed to protect me like Mama would if she were alive. Didn't much protect Lily or my mama, did it?" She took it off and laid it across the table, and the bells tinkled as they had on Lilah's anklet. I realized it was a charm bracelet, as Lilah's must have been. I hadn't gotten close enough to see how it was made. There was a small locket between the bells.

"You want to see somebody special? Here." She opened up the locket and showed me a tiny cutout of a woman's face. I realized it must be her mother. Her skin was pale beige, but her hair was Thelma's, and Miss Edna Sweets's; it fell long and loose around her pretty face.

"She's beautiful, isn't she?"

"Just like her daughter."

"She looks just like my Aunt Edna, except she looks white."

"Not really. Black women come in all kinds of different colors. That's what makes us so unique," I said.

She shook the bracelet gently.

"Aunt Edna says it's like they say in that movie, that whenever a bell rings, an angel gets her wings. Jimson Weed says there ain't no angels in this world, only devils."

"What does Jimson Weed know about angels or devils?" I said, and she gave me an impish grin.

"I guess you want to know what happened, don't you?" she said after a few minutes.

"Yeah, it's time you told me."

We sat there for another minute or so, then I said, "So you took Turk to the room where your mother died."

She looked away from me, talking to the table. "I did a very bad thing, Miss Hayle, and that's probably what the Lord was punishing me for, because I did a very bad thing."

"Taking Turk to your special place?"

"No. Something else."

"What?"

"I took Lily's baby. Lily didn't really want her, and she was so cute and everything, and Lily didn't really want to be a mother. When she came back in town, she was always leaving her with me anyway, so one day I just wouldn't give her back. Aunt Edna and I decided we'd keep her to teach Lily a lesson."

"But it was her child."

"But she didn't deserve her."

I sighed and let it go. At this point, it was water gone under the bridge and turned to mud.

"Then I talked to you that night, on Monday, and said I'd give her to Mr. Barnes, and then he called and I was supposed to bring her to his office, and then—"

"So you're saying that you called me, then spoke to Barnes, and you were going to take Baby Dal to his office, right?" She nodded. So Barnes had been telling the truth, or some of it anyway.

"Well, Mr. Barnes said he would give me some money, and my aunt really needs money for the house because it's old and coming apart, so I took the baby and was going to meet him like I said, and then I got scared and—"

"Why did you get scared?"

"Because of all the bad stuff folks say about him, how he's a crook and a murderer, and my Aunt Edna said once she thought he had something to do with Mama's death, and so I changed my mind, and I was scared to come home, because I knew you'd be there and would give her to him anyway.

"So I called my aunt and told her I wanted to take the baby to the place where Mama died, and maybe she'd tell me what to do. It's my mama's grandchild because it's Lily's, and that's how I ended up at the motel where Turk died."

I let her rest a minute, then turned in a different direction.

"How did you meet Turk?"

"He came by with Lily one of those times when she dropped off the baby. It was the first time I saw him, and he seemed real nice. When she went to the bathroom, he gave me his cell and said I should call him if I ever needed anything."

"Anything like what?"

She shrugged. "I don't know. I guess he kind of liked me, and, well, I thought he was kind of cute, and he was older and stuff, and—"

"So what did Lilah, Lily, have to say about that? You flirting with her man?"

"I wasn't flirting with him. He was flirting with me!"

"Him flirting with you, then."

"Nothing, 'cause she didn't see it. But when they left, he winked at me."

"Winked at you?"

"Yeah."

I rolled my eyes. My guess was that she had been attracted to the jerk like young girls sometimes are to men like that. But I was hardly the one to criticize her taste in men. "So you called him that Tuesday when you decided to get money from Barnes because you figured you needed protection," I said.

"Something like that."

"And then he met you at that motel, and he told you to call Barnes back because he figured out how the two of you could get more money from Barnes and still keep the baby, right?"

She nodded that I was right.

"And why did you want to keep the baby?"

"Because it belonged to my sister, and it was part of her."

"It never occurred to you that he could have something to do with her death?"

"You sound like a cop!"

"I used to be one. Answer the question."

"Why would it? He was nice to me. He was nice to the baby, at first."

All I could do was shake my head.

"So who killed Turk?"

"I don't know! He had me call Mr. Barnes back and tell him to come at midnight, just to be contrary and show him who was boss, and he said he would, and he told me to ask Mr. Barnes for a lot of money, and Mr. Barnes said he'd bring it, and so we started to wait.

"It was going on ten by then, and Baby Dal started crying, and Turk said if she didn't stop, he was going to hit her across the mouth. So I took her with me to get her something to eat, and he told us to be back in an hour, and I was."

"So you came back and he was dead?"

Her voice dropped to a whisper. "There was blood all over the room, Miss Hayle. On the floor, on the bed, in the bathroom—everywhere I looked, there was blood—and I tried to see if he was alive, but he wasn't, and I got blood all over me, so I grabbed the baby, slammed the door tight, and ran out as fast as I could."

She laid her head down on my table like a kid does at nap time.

"You took the baby to your Aunt Edna, and you came over here, right?"

She nodded that it was.

"How old are you, Thelma Lee?"

"Please call me Trinity."

"Trinity, then."

"I'm sixteen. I'll be seventeen soon."

I looked at Thelma Lee and thought about my son. Apparently, the Lord had added silly teenagers to the babies and fools He watched over.

"You tired?"

"I want to go to sleep and forget everything I saw. I been sleeping in your son's room. Is that okay?"

"I'm sure he wouldn't mind," I said. "But I want you to call your Aunt Edna before you go upstairs. When she came to my office today, she was worried sick about you."

"She came to your office? I called her when I was waiting for Mr. Barnes and told her where I was going to be, at the place Mama died. That's the only place I go. She knew where that was."

"Well, she was still worried about you. Because she came to see me this morning."

"I don't want her to be scared."

"Then call her. Now!"

"But she never answers the phone anyway."

"Then leave a message for her."

"Okay already, Miss Hayle! Jeez Louise!" she said, and I smiled because the tone of her voice, if not the expression, reminded me of my son.

I gave her the phone and nodded to the living room, and I could hear the warmth in her voice as she left her message.

"I'm going to go visit Mama's spirit tomorrow morning before I come home," I heard her say. "I love you, Auntie. I love you!"

"Thank you, Miss Hayle. I feel better now," she said after she hung up. "I'm going to go to bed now. I feel so safe here with you," she added.

"I'm glad you do," I said.

Still, I was uneasy about her, and I wasn't sure why. So before I went to bed that night, I locked my door and tucked my .38 under my pillow where I could get it quick. Just in case.

ELEVEN

T

HE GIRL WAS GONE THE NEXT MORNING. Jamal's bed was made, corners tucked in, pillow fluffed, and her towel and washcloth were hung neatly on the bathroom rack. On my refrigerator door, I found a letter on notebook paper stuck underneath a heart-shaped magnet.

Dear Miss Tamara Hayle,

I left when the sun came up first thing this morning.

I don't want nobody hurting you or your son. I could tell from his room he's a nice boy. He got a nice mama, too. Like mine was. I shoulda told you this, but I washed my clothes in the basement when I was here. They were real dirty (blood!). I used all your detergent, so I went and got you some more. The cheap kind. My aunt says it's all the same anyway. Hope that's okay. And, oh yeah, something else. My cell went dead, so I used your phone to call Mr. Treyman Barnes be-

fore you got home last night. Hope that's okay. I gotta make things
right for Baby Dal. She deserves to be with a rich granddaddy, not a
poor little aunt like me. It wasn't long distance!! You a real nice lady,
just like Lily said.

Your friend,
Trinity Sweets
(Thelma Lee)

I wished I could have done more for the girl, but that chance was
gone. I wondered how much Thelma Lee knew about her big sister.
Lilah had been hard on her "lame-ass, no-count baby sister," but there
had been an innocence about Thelma Lee, a sweetness that reminded
me of Lilah in our Jamaica days, and that memory made me shake my
head with sadness.

A fist straight through her throat. Fast and mean.

Thelma Lee wasn't that mean or I would have seen it.

Or would I?

What instinct had told me to tuck that gun beneath my pillow?
Truth be told, I wasn't sure about Thelma Lee. I didn't think she was
as naïve as she seemed. But I could be wrong about that, too. My
sense of myself as a reader of teenage minds had been seriously
shaken.

I'd never know now. The girl was gone wherever she was going,
and I had problems of my own.

I called Jamal on my cell phone before I left for work. I could tell
he was scared and worried. I hoped DeWayne was up to parenting

him like he needed, but I doubted it. DeWayne had always been good to his son, the best he could be, and Jamal was as central in De-Wayne's life, as much an anchor, as he was in mine. I didn't have the right to judge him.

"So, Mom, when can I come home?" Jamal asked before he hung up. "Can I come home Sunday? I miss you."

"We'll see about Sunday. Jake will be back on Monday, and I want to make sure you have a lawyer in case you need one."

"But the cops probably know where I am anyway."

"Yeah, they probably do," I agreed. "But they haven't been down there, and if you come home, they might be tempted to bring you in for questioning. I don't want you to go through that without a lawyer."

Dead silence.

"Jamal, you're breaking up. Are you still there?"

"Yeah, I'm here," he said, but the tone of his voice worried me. He sounded sulky and spoiled, not the kid I knew.

"Listen, Jake is in Toronto. I've left messages for him, and the minute he gets in town, he'll call."

"Maybe I should just tell them what I know."

"Not without a lawyer. And I want to find out more stuff anyway, about Lilah, about who could have killed her."

"Maybe I should just, you know, go away somewhere. Not wait for them to come, just hide out."

"Hide out? Hide out where? Are you out of your mind?" He was scaring the hell out of me. "Stay with your father, stay—"

"What if I just come home and hang out somewhere there? With some of the guys I know. We all look the same to the cops anyway.

They don't know one of us from another. We ain't nothing but nig-
gers to them anyway. We ain't shit!"

"Don't use language like that in my presence!"

"It's the truth!"

"Stop it!" I said, but my heart was pounding. "Not all cops are the
same. Think about your uncle Johnny."

"He's been dead a long time, Mom."

"Just stay where you are. Promise me, Jamal, that you'll stay with
your dad. Don't even think about coming up here now. Do you hear
me, Son? Please, Son, please!" It was the first time I'd ever begged him
for anything, and I didn't like the way the words sounded coming out
of my mouth. "Sunday. Somehow I'll find a way to bring you home by
Sunday. Sunday," I said again, and prayed I wasn't lying.

"I love you, Mommy."

Mommy. When was the last time I'd heard that? Ten years ago?
Jamal was DeWayne's anchor, and he was mine, too. But how much
anchoring could a teenager do? Jamal needed an anchor in his life, and
neither me nor DeWayne was able to be that for him, and the thought
of that made me ashamed.

As I was leaving the house, I noticed a sparkle of gold near the
sidewalk: Thelma Lee's charm bracelet. When I picked it up, the jingling bells reminded me of Lilah. I dropped it in my bag, double-
checked my locks, then glanced up at Jamal's window to make sure
she couldn't get in like that again. I'd give her a call when I got to work
and tell her I'd found it. The bracelet with her mother's picture in it
was important to her, and she was probably looking for it.

I wondered again about her story. There had been nothing in *The
Star-Ledger* or on TV about a brutal murder, and those kinds of

killings always lead the news. The paper was full of lottery winners, sports heroes, and class reunions. Nothing about a man named Turk Orlando in a notorious highway motel.

Could she have made the whole thing up? I only had her word that Turk was dead, and that she'd left the baby with her aunt. Sweet Thing had said she was covered with blood. But she hadn't mentioned the baby. Maybe she was up to something else. Maybe that bracelet was actually Lilah's anklet. I hadn't really gotten a good look at it. Was Thelma Lee an angel earning her wings or something else entirely?

Always the doubting Thomas. I had to laugh at myself. Maybe Jamal and Larry were right, that being a PI and imagining the worst of everybody was distorting my view of the world. The girl had gone from murder suspect to innocent victim to crazy teenager back to murder suspect in the space of twenty-four hours. My doubts about the girl were ridiculous, comical. But what if they weren't? Why had she trusted Turk Orlando so easily? Could they have been in it together from the jump, even when Lilah was alive? And when I listened to the message Matty Gilroy had left me, a chill went down my back, the kind that told me maybe I was right.

"Gilroy here. They found that guy, Turk, who killed that woman you asked about. He was the last call she made. They figure he met her, then murdered her. Found some jewelry that might have belonged to her on him, too. Case closed. No honor among thieves, ain't that the truth? Found his body over there in that motel off the highway. You know the one I'm talking about. How's your baby? Keep him where he is. Call me ASAP."

I collapsed in my chair. Should I call the cops? Confess everything I knew? Should I tell them that Thelma Lee had been there right after it happened and that she might be in danger? Or that maybe she was the killer. But then they would ask me about Jamal, and why I hadn't called them when she broke into my house.

Keep him where he is.

Matty knew more than she was saying. She couldn't betray her badge; she was as torn between her loyalty to a friend and the rule of law as I would be. *Keep him where he is* was all she dared say, and she hadn't said his name, just *your baby,* and that could mean anything to anybody who was listening. Her choice of words was deliberate, as if she were talking in code.

And what about Thelma Lee?

I played her message from Monday night again, listening closely to that high, little-girl voice crying about Baby Dal. She had been scared that night; she hadn't been able to hide it. I called the cell number she'd left and asked her to call me, then I tried Jersey City information and asked for the number of an Edna Sweets, but it was unlisted. I turned on my computer and tried to do some work, but the questions banging around in my head wouldn't let me be.

Had Turk Orlando been killed by the person who paid him to kill Lilah Love? He had been murdered around ten, according to Thelma Lee, two hours before Treyman Barnes was supposed to pick up the baby. But I had only Thelma Lee's word that Baby Dal had been there and that was the time of the murder. She could have lured Turk to the motel, killed him, then planted the jewelry on him. Maybe Sweet Thing and Jimson Weed had the baby all along. Maybe Turk had tried to double-cross her, and she'd killed him because of that, or maybe she killed him to avenge Lilah's death. Again, I wondered if Turk and Thelma Lee could have been in it from the beginning. Sixteen wasn't what it was even ten years ago. Sixteen would gleefully hang with a man twice her age and get the better of him quick. Turk had probably followed Lilah's advice about the older you get, the younger you fuck them . . . or try to. Or maybe it was somebody else who was playing a different game, another person working with Thelma for some reason impossible to know. And if that was the case, then who was next?

I jumped when the telephone rang, but I was glad to be distracted.

"You're talking to the new vice president of the esteemed Businessmen's Club of Newark, New Jersey," said Larry Walton on the other end.

He took me by surprise. The esteemed Businessmen's Club of Newark was so far from my mind, he could have been speaking in Hindi. "That's good news!" I managed to say.

"Unanimous. That's what the vote was, unanimous. You know what that means, don't you?"

"Why don't you tell me," I said, and he did for the next ten minutes. "Are we still on for tonight?" I asked with forced cheer.

"You don't sound too excited to me. Are you sure you still want to get together?" Larry said, picking up on my lack of enthusiasm; he was prone to sulk.

"Of course, I'm excited! And I have a surprise for you." Wvyetta's platinum package would come in handy.

"Okay, I'll see you tonight. Around eight. Oh yeah, I have something really important to talk to you about. Is Jamal still at his dad's? Be nice to have the place to ourselves."

I couldn't bring myself to answer.

"Good. See you then. Love you, Tam."

"Me, too," I said, the words stumbling out.

After he hung up, I called Gilroy to see if she had anything else about Turk's murder. She answered on the first ring.

"Gilroy here." I heard her light a cigarette, cough, then curse as she squashed it out, which made me smile.

"Hey Matty, it's me, Tamara Hayle. Give it up, girl. Those damn cigarettes are going to kill you."

"You don't think I been trying?" I chuckled at that, and she joined in, then stopped and turned serious. "You keeping the boy where he is?"

"Are they looking for him, Matty?" My voice was calm, but my heart had begun to pound.

"Like I said, they found some of the woman's jewelry on Turk, so they think he killed Lilah. He was also the last call she made."

"What about after that?"

"I don't know about after that. I just know what they told me. But nothing's sure until it's sure, you know what I mean? Look, Tamara, don't tell me where he is, I don't want to know, just make sure he has an alibi for this last one. That's the main thing."

"You don't seriously think somebody could suspect my son of this, do you?"

"Of course not! But I'm not seriously supposed to think anything, so don't tell me anything."

"How was Turk killed?"

"Hard. Execution-style. Cut his throat. Blood all over the place. A real slaughterhouse in there. But it was professional. Neat. One cut, deep and long. Walked up to him from behind, slaughtered him like you butcher a hog. Somebody knew what they were doing. Maybe it was payback for the way Love was killed, the throat thing."

"They should know there's no way in hell that a teenage boy—my teenage boy—could be even remotely involved in that kind of brutality," I said, incensed.

"You know it. I know it. But the cops don't know shit about you or your son. Look, a lot has happened in Jamal's life recently—all those killings in the city and everything—and except for the killer, he was the last person to see Lilah Love alive. He must have seen who killed her, even though he didn't realize it. They're still looking for more evidence. My bet is that they're going to probably pull him in as a material witness, but I know you don't want him involved in any of it, so just keep him where he is until they don't need to question him."

"Could the person who killed Turk have been a woman?"

"Possibly. A strong one. Big hands, big arms, good with a knife. Who knows? But she'd have to take him by surprise."

I hung up, her last words staying with me. I thought about Thelma Lee again, Trinity as she liked to call herself. Sipping tea, crying about her murdered mama and sister. Turk would have trusted her. He was a big man, and she was a woman. But what if she actually believed the role she liked to play, that of a karate-chopping, take-no-prisoners woman? *I got a knife, and I know how to use it,* she'd said. Why mention a knife as a possible weapon? She'd admitted being in the room with Turk; there had to be more to her story than she was telling. She had broken into my house late on Tuesday night. Could she have found something in Jamal's room—on his computer—that would tell her where he was? Could he be in danger?

I called DeWayne's house and finally got him on his cell.

"Where you been? I been trying to call you for the last forty minutes," DeWayne yelled into my ear. "Do you know where your son is? I been driving around here for the last hour looking for him."

"I just spoke to him. He's with you!"

"No he's not. I don't know where the hell he is! I had a, you know, an appointment, and when I got back—"

"Are you telling me that you left that boy by himself to see one of your sluts! What the fuck is wrong with you?"

"Now, Tamara, ain't no need to be calling nobody out her name. Boy probably took a walk or something. I don't know. You said you just talked to him, right? Then he's okay."

"No, he's not okay! The goddamn cops could pick him up. Whoever killed Lilah Love and Turk could be looking for Jamal! How could you let this happen?" I was shaking so badly I could scarcely hold the phone, so I put it down for a minute. I didn't want to hear anything DeWayne had to say. But I heard him anyway.

"Listen to me! What did he say when you spoke to him? What did he say?"

"He said he wanted to come home," I finally said, as calmly as I could. It didn't do any good to keep yelling at him. He was as scared as me.

"I didn't give him much money and he can't get a bus from here, so he ain't coming home," DeWayne said. "Look, I saw him this morning, and he seemed okay. He answered your call, that's the important thing. Call him again, and I'll keep calling, too. Okay? And maybe you should try to find out who did this shit and got him in this mess in the first place. Maybe you should try to do that so he can come back home with you where he belongs. And I wasn't with no woman," he added before he hung up.

Woman, slut—I didn't give a good goddamn. All I knew was my son was in danger, and I didn't know where he was. DeWayne Curtis was right about one thing, though. I had to find out who did this shit and get Jamal out of this mess as soon as I could. DeWayne Curtis had been damned right about that.

Thelma Lee had to be the key to this whole thing. She was the one who had taken the child and brought this hell down on everybody. I needed to talk to her again, ask direct questions about both murders, get more details about her relationship with her older sister and with Turk. I had real facts about the killing now, and I'd be able to grill her and get some answers. She thought I was acting like a cop at my house; she hadn't seen nothing yet. I knew I'd be able to tell if she was lying, and if she wasn't, I'd help her remember something she may have forgotten.

I don't want nobody hurting you or your son.

Had she been talking about herself? I needed to go back to Jersey City and get a sense of where things were. I could talk to Sweet Thing then, too, and find out if she had the baby like Thelma had said.

It was rush hour, so it was six before I pulled up in front of Sweet Thing's house. Before I could ring the bell, Jimson Weed came running out of the house and onto the sagging porch. I thought about the way he'd spit on my floor and got disgusted all over again, but if I was hoping for some kind of an apology, I was a bigger fool than he.

"You can stop right there. Don't you come nowhere near this house. Nowhere near it. We don't need your help."

"So Thelma Lee is home?" I peeked over his shoulder and spotted Sweet Thing peeking from behind a shade in the living room.

"We got all we need. We a family. We got each other, and that's all you need to know."

"So I take it Thelma Lee is here?"

"Just go on back where you come from."

"I know you have Lilah's baby. Thelma Lee told me that."

"Thelma Lee didn't tell you nothing!"

"If Thelma Lee is here, I want to talk to her." I paused for a moment, wondering whether I should go on, then said, "You must know by now that Lilah, the girl you call Lily, is dead."

He stopped short and glanced at the window, then looked back at me. "I know."

"Would you tell Sweet Thing that I'm sorry for her loss?"

"I'll tell her."

"But I want to talk to Thelma Lee, and I need to know that Lilah's baby is okay."

"All we want to do is be a family, live like a family in peace and quiet like, but you folks just won't let us alone, will you? I got to look out for my woman like she's always looked out for me. I can't have no one making her upset, do you understand me?" His eyes pleaded with me as strong as his words, and I finally began to understand.

"Here, please take this," I said, giving him Thelma Lee's bracelet. "Will you please give this back to Thelma Lee? It's very precious to her and she left it at my house. It has a picture of her mother in it."

"I know what it's got in it," he said as he carefully folded it into his handkerchief and stuffed it in his pocket. "Don't worry, I'll make sure she gets it." He said it with a kindly nod and slight smile that struck me as surprisingly caring, and I liked him better for it. "Good evening, Ms. Hayle." He went back inside, spoke to Sweet Thing, and pulled down the shade where Sweet Thing had been standing, and for the first time, I felt compassion, which surprised the hell out of me.

Jimson Weed wasn't really a puzzle to me; I'd known men like him all my life. My father's friends, mostly, who had fought in Vietnam like he had and come home to deal with their wounds and American racism. It was too much for some of them to endure; souls scar easily, and they became lost men, drinking or drugging and so caught up in their own misery they couldn't see you when you looked straight at them. Jimson Weed had been one of those men until Sweet Thing became his salvation. She had rescued him from his grief, and he had dedicated himself to her well-being. He was lucky to have an anchor in his life. Larry Walton was one of my anchors, and I was lucky to have him, too.

WAS DOWN ROUTE 1-9 when I finally got Jamal on my cell phone, and I pulled into a gas station so we could talk. I didn't want to make things worse than they were, so I played the calm, understanding mom.

"Hey, Jamal, where you been?" I said, casual as could be.

"You're mad, huh?" He knew me too well.

"Where were you?" I snapped, all pretense gone.

"I'm okay."

"I didn't ask *how* you were. I asked *where* you were."

"I'm home now. Not home, but here with Dad," he corrected himself. "I just needed to get out, spend some time by myself. You want to talk to him? He's watching the game."

"No."

"Mom?"

"Yeah, Son."

"I can't see why I can't come home now."

"You know as well as I do. I told you to stay where you are."

"Okay." He didn't sound convinced. "Do you want to talk to Dad?"

"No, I told you that. I'm just really worried about you, Son."

"Don't worry about me, Mom; I'm fine." He chuckled then, and the sound of his laughter made me smile. "That's what you always say to me, isn't it? 'I'm fine, Son; don't worry.' Don't *you* worry. Everything's going to work out okay."

"You think so?" That was what he always asked me.

"I know so." He tossed back what I always said back.

"You're really okay, then?"

"I'm fine. Fine!" His voice was strong and assured, and I realized how quickly he was becoming a man. Too quickly. "Hey, Mom. Take a deep breath. Relax. Okay?"

"Okay," I said, and did what he suggested. He did sound fine, and he was safe. At least for now. Worrying didn't solve a damn thing.

As I got back on the road, I thought about Larry Walton and everything he meant to me—and everything he didn't.

I wondered about the "important" thing he wanted to ask me. In the past few months, he'd been hinting about getting married, or, as he put it, "formalizing our relationship." I wasn't sure if I was ready for marriage, but he was the kind of man who would want an answer quickly if he asked. I knew I had to be prepared to give him one or I would lose him.

Good men were hard to come by, especially the older I got, and Larry Walton was a good man. I could see myself settling down with him and living very well. I could make a nice piece of change off of my house (not Jersey City prices, but more than I had now) and move into his charming West Orange house. He had mentioned sending

Jamal to a boarding school, which I didn't agree with, but we would compromise on that. As his wife, life would be sweet and easy. And what would I be giving up?

Sweet Thing came to mind and the way Jimson Weed had yanked that window shade down in front of her face. I remembered the way he'd stood ramrod-stiff in front of her like a soldier protecting her from an enemy. What had she given up for the protection he offered?

I picked up some food for dinner—steaks, salad, baking potatoes. Larry was a man of simple tastes. And I stopped by Whole Foods for a chocolate mousse cake and a good liquor store for some expensive red wine. When I got home, I cleaned up the place, burned some incense, lit candles in strategic nooks, and after a luxurious bubble bath, slipped into the sexiest thing I owned and waited, willing and eager for my man to walk through the door.

It was going on ten o'clock when he finally showed up. "Willing and eager" had disappeared at eight forty-five.

"You're late," I said the obvious, as he handed me a dozen wilted pink roses he'd probably picked up at the A&P.

"Tamara, I'm so sorry about this. Something important came up, and I had to stop by the club. I'll make it up to you, I promise." He obviously felt bad about it, so I smelled the roses, gave him a kiss, and let it go. He gave me one of his winning grins.

Larry Walton was a man who people trusted the moment he grinned. I certainly had when I ran into him after high school, more years ago than I care to admit, and when he sold me my latest car. He was a kind man, too, always had been, and that was what had drawn me to him. Like my ex-husband, he took clothes very seriously—

shoes, jewelry, anything that whispered success—although his success, unlike DeWayne Curtis's, was real. He was well built and well kept, as Wyvetta had observed once, spotting him from afar, and he had a cute dimple that always won me over. He was, as my friend Annie said, the three "Ss" that a good husband must be: steady, sturdy, settled.

We sipped some wine, ate some dinner, nibbled at the cake, drank more wine, finally snuggled close to each other on the living room couch. I curled up next to him and laid my head on his shoulder. He kissed my forehead, then my lips.

"Oh, I almost forgot," I said, remembering the platinum certificate from Wyvetta's shop. "I think you'll enjoy this!" I had put it upstairs in the drawer of my night table, not sure whether I wanted to present it to him before or after we made love. This seemed the right moment, considering that our evening had gotten off to a rocky start. I ran upstairs, two steps at a time like Jamal, pulled it out of my drawer, and dashed back down. I handed it to him grinning, as bashful as a kid. The moment he glanced at it, I knew I'd made a mistake.

Wyvetta had overdone it with the gold box and silver bow, topped by a fake white carnation. I'd been so involved worrying about meeting Treyman Barnes, I hadn't thought twice about the flower until I handed it to him. He took it, smiled graciously, but examined it critically.

"Looks like something from Wyvetta Green's shop," he said. He must have noticed how my face fell because he quickly added as he placed it on the table, "Nice. Thanks, baby. This was thoughtful."

"Aren't you going to open it?"

"Sure," he said, but I could tell it was an afterthought. He slowly opened the box, then read the card aloud. In her haste to make a sale, Wyvetta, never much of a speller, had misspelled certain key words.

This entitles one gentleman to an afternoon of delite at the Beauty Biscuit compliment of Wyvetta Green and Company. Included— head message with special oils, hair cut, pedicure, etc. etc.

"Message? What kind of message is she offering?"

"She meant to write *massage*."

"So what's the 'etc. etc.,' or dare I ask?"

"If you don't like it, I'll take it back," I snapped.

"No, no. I like it, I like it. Who in his right mind wouldn't want to spend an afternoon in the Beauty Biscuit surrounded by all that pink and purple with Wyvetta Green and company rubbing oil onto his head?"

I pulled away from him. "I hate it when you're like this," I said.

"Like what?"

"Nasty and judgmental."

"Hey, don't be that way, baby!" He tried to kiss me. "I'm really sorry. It's a great gift, but it's really not my style." I pulled away from him again. I'd known Wyvetta a long time, and I didn't like anyone making fun of her, not even in jest.

"*Now* what's wrong?"

"Nothing. I just don't like you putting down my friend."

He was the one to pull away now. "To be real honest, I've never understood your friendship with Wyvetta Green anyway. You're a very classy woman, Tamara. You're smart, independent, lovely, with a good business head. Those are some of the reasons I've fallen in love with you. I could take you anywhere in this world with me, anywhere, and you'd know how to behave, what to wear, how to act, for crying out loud. We're a good team, the two of us. We can reach all of our goals. But Wyvetta Green? I have nothing in common with her or Eric. I haven't seen a gold tooth like that in a man's mouth since my uncle Horace died."

"Earl. His name is Earl," I said.

"Your choice of friends reflects who you are. They're like the clothes you wear or the car you drive. I could no more take people like them to a function at the Businessmen's Club than I could—"

"Are you telling me that my friends aren't good enough for you?" I didn't like where this was going.

"No, of course not, baby. Your friend Annie, and that guy she's married to, the Nigerian guy, they're the kind of people . . . well, that can bring good things into our lives. I could see us going out to dinner together, traveling, but Wyvetta and Earl? Well, you know what I'm trying to say."

"No, I don't know what you're trying to say."

Larry took my hand and gently touched it with his lips. "What I'm saying is that I really want to take our relationship, well, to a different level. That will mean that we'll both have to let parts of us go to get there. That's what marriage is about, sacrificing bits of yourself for the greater good."

"And Wyvetta Green and Earl are the parts of me that you want to sacrifice?"

Larry kissed my hand again, then let it drop. He picked up the wine and gulped it down. "Look, I'm not asking you to cut her off, just . . . well, just don't have her in your life as much. What does she really offer you besides a free perm every now and then in that tacky little beauty shop over on—"

"That 'tacky little beauty shop' is right under my tacky little office," I said.

"I didn't mean it like that. All I'm saying is sometimes in life, you have to let people go—not all at once, but bit by bit. You go on to better things, and sometimes . . . well, old friends don't fit into the world you're entering."

"The world inhabited by members of the Businessmen's Club of which you've just been elected vice president and that wouldn't have me as a member!"

"I'm going to do something about that," he said, not looking me in the eye.

"But would never accept Wyvetta with her tacky little shop or Earl with his gold tooth," I continued.

"You know that's the truth as well as I do," he said.

We sat there for the next ten minutes, close to each other but not touching. I thought about Wyvetta and all the things we'd been through together and about Larry and how good he made me feel, but I couldn't think of anything to say to make things right, so we sat there, finishing off the bottle of wine in silence. He opened another one and poured me a glass.

"Larry," I said after a few minutes, "when we spoke earlier, you said you had something to discuss with me." My words sounded heavy and formal, as if I were speaking to a business associate. "What exactly was it?"

"Do you really want to know?" His eyes told me he felt as bad as I did about the way things were unfolding.

"Yeah, I do."

"I'm almost afraid to say it now," he said with a half grin, and for a moment, I fell in love with him again.

"Tell me." I returned his smile. There might be hope for this evening yet.

"Well, I ran into Treyman Barnes at the—"

"Treyman Barnes!"

"Yeah, and I know you've had some dealings with him, and I—"

"W-who told you I had dealings with him?" I stammered out.

"Well, I don't want to go into it, but I want to remind you that he's not like some of those lowlifes you run into in your business. He's a gentleman, a class act, and an important contributor to the community."

Then you working for the Devil.

"Not everybody feels that way, that Treyman Barnes is such a class act, such an upstanding citizen, believe me," I said.

"Well, the important people do, and ultimately, they're the ones who count, right?" He said it with a playful wink, meant to soften the words, but it didn't.

"So now you're trying to tell me how to run my business."

"You know I would never do that." He looked genuinely hurt, and that made me feel bad. "Hey, baby, I can't say nothing right tonight, can I?"

"I've got a lot on my mind."

"So when is my favorite guy coming back?" he said after a moment, trying to change the subject. He knew that the mere mention of my son always made me smile. But it didn't this time, and he studied my face and then shook his head. "Look, don't worry about Jamal. He is having big fun down there with his dad, and maybe we can have some fun of our own without prying teenage eyes."

"My son's eyes don't pry, and I miss him," I said as evenly as I could.

"Well, why don't you tell him to come home?"

"It's not time yet."

He nodded and smiled. "Maybe it's for the best, Tamara. I know you don't think much of the man, but sometimes a father is the only one who can give a boy like Jamal the guidance he needs."

"A boy like Jamal?"

"Well, you know what I mean. He's been dealing with a lot of bad stuff recently. The death of that kid he knew, your block going bad. He talks back a lot, too; I've been noticing that. It's only a matter of time before he starts hanging with the wrong kids, getting into trouble with the cops, and then it's over, forget it. Ain't nothing you can do once the cops get hold of him. You know how it goes for black men. Once they arrest you, for anything, your life ain't worth shit. A firm hand for a couple of months, maybe even a year or two, will do that boy a world of good."

"And you actually believe that DeWayne Curtis, my trifling ex-husband, is the firm hand my son needs?"

"Well, the firm hand's not mine, Jamal has made that pretty clear, and he's got to have a man in his life, sooner rather than later, I'd say."

Was Larry right? I wondered, beginning to doubt myself. Jamal had, after all, gotten into that car with that crazy bitch in the first place. I didn't say anything for a while, and then said as gently as I could, "I need to be by myself tonight, baby. I need to think some things through."

Puzzled, he studied my face. "By yourself? Didn't you invite me over?"

"I know. I'm sorry, but there's a lot going on in my life now, and I need to sort things out."

"It's that damn job, isn't it? It's dangerous and it's unseemly. I can't sleep at night worrying what kind of hoodlum is going to drop into your office and what he's going to do you. It's not what I want a woman I love to do for a living.

"I want to protect you, Tamara, from everything and everyone that can hurt you, but you seem bent on living your life on the edge. We've talked about this before, and I need an answer. When are you going to find another way to make a living?"

"I'm not," I said.

We sat together in an uneasy silence. Larry turned on the TV, and we spent fifteen minutes watching a doc about offshore banking on PBS. Finally, he sighed and we kissed good night as the friends we were. I promised I would call him the next morning, and I knew that I would. But I hadn't been able to tell him what was really on my mind, and that said something troubling about our relationship.

After he left, I changed into jeans and a sweatshirt and, suddenly exhausted, collapsed on the couch, wondering what the hell was wrong with me. When the phone rang, I jumped to get it, assuming it was Larry, hoping it was Jamal. It was Basil Dupre.

"Listen, Tamara, I know what you said, and I respect that, but I'm leaving town sooner than I expected. I came back to the States to see you, to be honest, and I want to be able to say a decent goodbye before I leave. I don't know when I'm coming back. So what are you doing tonight?"

"Nothing," I said, and burst into laughter.

THIRTEEN

ASIL DIDN'T ASK WHY I was laughing, and I didn't tell him. Mostly, it was the ironies—of Larry taking off like he had and me not telling him the truth, of being so sure about life on Monday and watching it turn to shit in four days, about Basil Dupre after months of no word.

I argued with myself for ten minutes, one moment deciding to tell Basil to forget it, the next simply accepting my fate. I rode with fate. I was, after all, a grown woman fully in charge of myself, and there was no reason why the man couldn't drop by for a visit. I'd known him for nearly fifteen years, and despite our past, we had no future. Truth was, my "future" had just walked out the door, chased by my big mouth and bad attitude.

And maybe I had a third option: Cancel Basil. Call Larry. Apologize for being a bitch. But what would I say? That I agreed with his bullshit about my profession? That Jamal really was better off with DeWayne? That Wyvetta and Earl weren't good enough for our "new" life? And what would I say to Basil? Sorry. Made a mistake. Forget it. Catch you on the rebound.

The best thing to do was nothing—let the game play itself out. The no-brand-name lights in my kitchen cast the room and everyone in it in a greenish glare that made conversation reminiscent of an interview in a police interrogation room. What could go wrong in a place like this?

Basil was an old friend who respected my boundaries. We'd stick to business if I made that clear. I had some questions about Treyman Barnes, and Basil could answer them. If Barnes was even remotely connected to Lilah's death, I might be able to convince the cops to roll down *that* avenue. They probably wouldn't want to spotlight the great Citizen Barnes, but it would give them somebody to chew on besides me and Jamal. Basil would also know if Turk had ever worked for Barnes, and that would tie him closer. No way Barnes could kill Turk, but Basil might know of some muscle he could hire to do it. And there was also Thelma Lee aka Trinity Sweets to consider.

One cut, deep and long. Walked up to him from behind, slaughtered him like you butcher a hog.

A woman could kill like that, Gilroy had said. And there had been blood on Thelma Lee's clothes, she'd written that herself, and she'd washed and dried them in my machine. It would be just my damn luck for the cops to find traces of Turk Orlando's DNA in my old-as-dirt Maytag.

I should have called the cops from the get.

But what good would that have done? They were looking for killers, not Baby Dal and a missing teenager. And where was Baby

Dal? Had Thelma really made "things right" for her by giving the child to Treyman Barnes like she said she would do in that note? What would Treyman Barnes do to her if she had—or hadn't?

Basil might have thoughts on that part of it, too, especially when I told him that Jamal was involved. Basil had never met my son or spoken more than a few words to him on the phone, but he had watched Jamal grow up through my stories and observations. I'd told him about Jamal's first day of school, when he made the debate team in fifth grade and tried out for junior varsity. He was the one to suggest that Jamal learn capoeira, a Brazilian form of martial arts and self-defense as graceful as it was deadly. He cared about Jamal and did what he could to help us when we needed it. I'd mentioned in passing that Jamal had fallen in love with computers, and a new Mac had mysteriously appeared on our front porch two days later. A winter wardrobe materialized out of nowhere when money was tight, and a red dirt bike dropped out of the sky on Jamal's thirteenth birthday. Jamal always assumed that his father was his benefactor, and much to my disgust, DeWayne, with a wink and a smile, took undeserved credit.

I never told Jamal the true origin of these gifts. I knew instinctively that he would disapprove of my outlaw boyfriend and object to our relationship. From the moment he outgrew me, he was determined to protect me, and he would deem Basil's lifestyle a threat. I knew it was best to keep my relationship with him away from the prying eyes of my overprotective son. So Basil remained one of my guilty, secret pleasures, along with gulping too much red wine, pigging out on Lindt chocolate, and nonstop movies on the Lifetime Movie Network.

Anything you need I will do, Basil had told me earlier this week, and I needed answers from him, that was all. But when the doorbell rang, my heart beat like it had the first time he kissed me.

It is my sad lot in life to end up with men who dress better than me, and Basil Dupre was no exception. He wasn't a show-off like De-Wayne Curtis, with his Gucci suits and Bruno Magli loafers, nor did he "dress for success" like Larry. His tastes were subtle and his clothes well chosen—casually elegant. His tailored steel gray shirt set off his beautiful skin and caught the glimmer of the platinum Rolex that peeked out from the cuff. His dark blue slacks were topped by a leather belt, lizard, crocodile, or some other exotic skin I couldn't identify. (Basil was many things; conservationist was not one of them.) For a moment, I wished I'd changed into something more fetching, then remembered why he was here.

"I wanted to see you before I left. Thank you," he said gravely, and delivered a brief kiss to my forehead. I liked the way he smelled. Not overpowering with perfume but a scent that made me breathe him in and enjoy it. "I don't know when I'll be back this way." He glanced around my kitchen. "Nice room, Tamara. A good feel to it," he added, with a shy smile that made me wonder if he was as unsure of himself as me.

"Practical," I said.

"No-nonsense," he clarified.

"I was going to make some tea. Do you want some?"

"Sure. Sounds good."

I put on the kettle and got out matching cups and saucers, the china ones that had belonged to my grandmother, then sat down across from him. I saw my kitchen as he must see it—the dull yellow walls in need of a fresh coat of paint, the out-of-date calendar on the wall, the ancient oven and worn black-and-white checkered linoleum. Old and worn was what this room was, but for me it was the most comfortable one in the house. I'd done little to it in the years since my family had died. Maybe because it reminded me of them, the good as well as the bad, and I couldn't bring myself to change it. I thought for a moment of Sweet Thing and her old house, and understood her love for it. Old things have memories, she'd told Thelma Lee. The same thing went for old friends, old loves.

The kettle whistled, and I poured water into the teapot and dropped in the tea ball filled with the loose tea Annie had brought me back from South Africa. Rooibos, it was called, and I was nearing the end of it. It was strong without being bitter and had a unique, distinctive taste. I let it brew for a moment, then poured us both a cup and brought it to the table.

"This is a well-made table," Basil said, stroking the surface with his slender, elegant fingers. "Strong and beautiful, like its owner."

"I didn't know you were into furniture."

"I love beautiful things," he said with a half smile.

"Old, too?" I ignored his compliment.

"Good wood always grows more beautiful with age. You've had it awhile?"

"I bought it after I left DeWayne," I said, then wished I hadn't because it brought back the first time I'd met him. He'd been an acquaintance of DeWayne's then, but not after our kiss. Did he remember it, too?

The dark red tea smelled like flowers, and its exotic fragrance filled the space between us. Basil smiled with pleasure at first taste. "Rooibos. So you like this one, too, do you? I'll bring you some back next time I'm in Johannesburg."

"So you've been to South Africa?"

He smiled, nodding slightly, glanced away for a moment. "Not for a while."

"Business or pleasure?"

"Business, but pleasure always comes first."

The very mention of the word brought back our last time together. Should I have left this final goodbye unsaid?

"Your son, is he still with his father?"

My thoughts swung back to my kitchen. "Yes."

"And he's coming back soon?" I avoided his eyes and nodded, but he knew I was hiding something. He reached across the table, easily took my face in hand, and tipped it up so I couldn't avoid his eyes.

"Tell me what's happened." His eyes wouldn't let me lie.

"You sure you want to hear it?"

"Of course I do."

So I told him all of it, about Lilah Love and Baby Dal, where the story began and would probably end. I described how brutally Lilah had been murdered, and why Jamal's ill-timed ride in her car had made him at least a material witness and at most a suspect or possible victim. I described Turk, dead now, and Thelma Lee, gone but not forgotten. I explained how I suspected the killings were somehow tied to Treyman Barnes, and I ended with a long-winded, guilty confession— about how what I did for a living had endangered my son, and that the man I was involved with was probably right about me, that I was a lousy mother, a careless person, and that my son was better off living with his father. My final words were followed by a childish sob it was impossible to disguise.

"So who is this man who would say these things to you?" Basil asked, indignant.

"Larry. My used-to-be boyfriend."

"Used to be?" A slight smile crossed his lips.

"He left earlier tonight."

"Tonight? He must be a fool, then," he said with chuckle, which made me feel better. "He must not know you as I do to say such foolish things. You're better off without him."

"And better off with somebody like you?" The words were out of my mouth before I knew it. "We both know that's not real."

"You said it, not me."

"Basil, it's impossible between us. You know that as well as I do."

"Perhaps you're right," he said, and I was surprised by how quickly my stomach dropped, the disappointment that came from nowhere. "But I will tell you this, Tamara. Think of your son, and judge yourself. You know what kind of woman you are, how strong and how good. Now think of DeWayne Curtis, and we both know what he is. Tell me that Jamal is not better off with you, and always will be. As for your work?" He grinned and shrugged. "You're like me, Tamara. You are smart and capable. You take the hand you're dealt, and you play it with all you've got; win or lose, you never fold. You are a survivor, as am I."

I gave him a half nod, touched by this burst of cheerleading.

"You need . . . let me say, spice in your life. You're no dull, bland woman who bores a man before he knows it. If that's what he wants, tell him to find one of those silly, insipid women afraid of their own shadows. He doesn't deserve what he's got."

I dropped my eyes, not sure if I wanted to look into his.

"Look at me," he said gently. "I need to tell you this. Things between us may be impossible now, but not for always, I'm sure of that. I always come back to you."

"Sooner or later."

"But always."

"And when will you come back this time?" The question was more demand than question, and he chose not to answer, sipping his tea instead.

"How do I help you protect your son?"

"By telling me everything you know about Treyman Barnes."

"Treyman Barnes? That isn't his style. To have some woman killed like that in a car. When he did those kinds of things, he was smart about it."

"And he did do those kinds of things?"

Basil shrugged, said nothing.

"But what if he wanted something she had, like the baby? Could he be that ruthless?"

"He'd find another way to get it. He's not a stupid man."

"What about Turk?"

"The muscle with the girl?"

"The one whose throat was cut."

"A messy way to kill a man," he said with a shudder. I didn't ask him how he knew.

"What if Turk killed Lilah on his orders, and he had him killed by someone else to cover his tracks?"

"Why bother? If it came to that, nobody would believe Turk over Treyman Barnes. There would be no need to cover his tracks. Barnes isn't strong enough to kill like that, and he couldn't hire a man to do that kind of killing. That killing was a personal one. There's something missing in a man who kills like that. It's not like on TV, Tamara. Killing is hard, and it always takes a bit of your soul. Even if it's justified."

"I know that," I said defensively.

"No, you don't, not really," he said, glanced away, not willing to meet my eyes. He leaned back in the chair slightly, studying me. "What else do you want to know?"

"Why you were there that day, when I saw you on Monday."

"Business. I thought I told you."

"What kind of business, Basil?"

He hesitated just long enough to make me think he wasn't going to tell me, then his voice softened.

"I knew Treyman Barnes from the old days, Tamara, and he's changed since then. I'm not sure how much, but he's not what he once was. I met him through his father, who knew my uncle. They shared some . . . business."

"Business. Always business," I said, amused.

"What can I tell you?" he grinned, innocent eyes.

"His father was definitely a stone-cold gangster," I said, recalling Miss Peterson's words.

"As was uncle."

"As are you?"

"Shall we not go there?"

"And he's not now, you're saying." I brought it back to Treyman Barnes.

"He was once, or so they say, and if he still is, he keeps it to himself."

"Then what did he want from you?" I wasn't sure I'd get it. He was always circumspect when it came to "business."

"He asked me for some advice." He paused a moment, took a sip of tea, which told me he was only willing to go so far. "Nothing to do with this Lilah Love you mentioned. About something in another part of the world. You say you met her in Jamaica?"

"The time I saw you down there," I said, and it all came back in a swirl of memory—the brightness of the sun and the smell of the sea and the feel of crisp white sheets in the villa where we made love.

"Good time we had there, eh?"

A rush of heat shot through me.

"You should come to Johannesburg with me. For some more of this." He poured himself another cup of tea. "And that." He alluded to Jamaica.

"Tell me more about Treyman Barnes." I stuck to the subject.

"What more is there to tell?"

"You said he was once in this . . . business you don't want to talk about."

He smiled, said nothing.

"You said you would tell me, now do it." I turned tough, but it made him chuckle, which was not the response I expected, then he turned serious again.

"Now, I'll tell you this, Tamara. They say a few years back he was involved in some dealings over on Avon Avenue that ended badly, and they say what happened that night was what changed him, and that kind of thing can change a man."

I remembered Miss Peterson's words.

"And years before that, when he was a young man, very young, he made his money off of women, as they say. His father was responsible for that. But that was before my time. It is a filthy business, and he's out of it now. I would never have dealings with such a man."

"I'm relieved to hear that."

"Tamara, who do you take me for?"

"Exactly who you are," I said.

"And what is that?"

"If you don't know by now, I'm not going to tell you," I said, which made him smile.

"Come out with me," he said. "We'll have some dinner, a bit of wine, come back here. See where things lead."

"Not on your life, because we know where things lead," I said, but even as I said it, I was considering it. What would it take, I asked myself, to go out and have dinner and a drink with this man one last time? What harm could it do?

"I'd gladly give my life for more of your time." It was such an obvious, clumsy attempt at seduction it made me laugh, not the hysterical laughter of yesterday afternoon but light and carefree. He watched me for a moment, then he laughed, too.

"It's good to see you laugh," he said.

"It's good to do it."

We sat there for a while, sipping tea and avoiding each other's eyes, until he said, "It's time for me to go. I'll see you when I see you." He reached across the table, took my hand, held it for a moment. I was surprised by the finality in his voice, that things were finished between us. I stood with him, suddenly not so sure I wanted things to end like this, even though I had insisted they should.

"And you are sure of this?" He asked that question that had come to me, too.

"I don't know." It was the most honest thing I could say.

"Neither do I," he said. "But I'll leave now. I don't want to make things more difficult. Do you want me to stay?" he asked in the same breath. I said nothing because I didn't know the answer. His smile was a sad one as he walked toward the door; then he suddenly turned to face me.

"Do you remember the first time I kissed you?" he asked.

It was the first time we'd met. A kiss for the bride, he'd told De-Wayne half teasing, but something had happened, his body so dangerously close it had changed us both. DeWayne had watched us embrace, too outraged to react. It had been said as a joke, but we both knew when I stepped away from him how things would be.

I nodded, committing to nothing but that memory.

"Goodbye," he said, and pulled me to him halfway to the door, and when he kissed me, this one last time, everything came back in a rush as it always did, and I couldn't pull away.

I had always enjoyed kissing him. For hours once, we had kissed, gently and leisurely, nothing touching except our lips, a teasing seduction that seemed to go nowhere until it exploded into a frenzy of passion. Yet this was not like that day but rather like that first time so many years ago, when I was curious about him, then astonished. I allowed myself to be drawn into that kiss, to feel the pleasure of him against me, his lips and tongue touching mine. My body had its own memory.

We pulled away, both of us breathless, and gazed at each other for an instant.

"How far shall we go with this?" he whispered.

"We have no commitment to each other. How far can things go?"

He gently kissed my forehead. "Don't you know by now that you and I are beyond that?"

MY BEDROOM WAS DARK when we entered it, but light filtering in from the hall threw a soft sheen on the pale blue walls. The incense I'd burned earlier in anticipation of my evening with Larry still lingered. I'd chosen lavender, a fragrance of healing Wyvetta had told me, because I felt that Larry and I were in need of that. And Basil, I wondered, as I pulled him close to me. Did we need healing as well?

I'd put my fancy sheets on my bed this morning, the six-hundred-thread-count ones that had cost me more than a trip to Wyvetta's. The price had outraged me when I slid my debit card through the machine, but now I understood. They felt like good silk against my naked skin. For a moment, I felt a twinge of guilt about Larry. I'd assumed he'd be lying beside me tonight, but when Basil touched me, caressing me as gently as any man ever had, nothing else mattered but the thought of having him inside me. In that moment, I forgot my decision that there would be nothing between us; I just felt the sheer excitement of having his touch on my thighs, my breast.

His body was more muscular than I remembered. I had forgotten the shape of his shoulders, the small of his back, the way the scar on his chest broke his smooth skin with its rough edge. I ran my lips over it, enjoying the feel of it, the brisk, salty taste of him against my tongue. Things started easily between us, as they always did. Short, simple kisses growing in urgency until there was nowhere for them to go but other places on our bodies. I had forgotten how good we were together, how thrilling it was to finally have him enter me.

I have never been a woman who could make love to a man without a deeper connection; my heart was forever tied to my body. There were times when I wished that tie would break, but it never did. De-Wayne was my first real lover, and there had been many men since him; each one had meant more to me than I cared to remember. But no one touched my heart or body like Basil did; no one could touch places within me that only he seemed to know to touch. I was frightened by how much I felt for him, how much he made me feel.

And when I lay beside him, both of us tired and breathless, I remembered how he had felt inside me and knew by what was in his eyes when he smiled that he did, too. I wondered then about things between us and realized that nothing else mattered. I was as sure of that as I was of anything else.

You know me as no other woman does, he had told me that day at Barnes's office. How true that was, I'd never know. I only knew what was true for me, and that was that he knew *me* as no other man did, and that it was as if he had never left me.

His flight to somewhere left from Kennedy early the next morning, and I woke at midmorning with the memory of him still on my skin. The note on my pillow said to call him about Jamal, and that he would be in touch with me on Sunday to see how things were. I smiled when I read that.

I wasn't sure what our night said about me and Larry Walton. I hoped I'd know when I saw him again. But I knew what it said about me and Basil. We were back where we started, neither of us sure where that was.

FOURTEEN

WYVETTA PEEKED OUT OF HER SHOP as I headed to my office the next morning, and a grin quickly replaced the frown that had been on her face.

"Well, I see you got your money's worth. You been right sad walking around here. A good night of loving do bring a change of attitude in a woman's life, don't it?"

"Huh?"

Wyvetta laughed. "Don't play cute with me, Tamara. I'd say that platinum certificate you bought for your man was worth every penny. Tell him he can come anytime he wants for his treatments. Early or late. Any day of the week. A man who can put a smile like that on a woman's face this early in the morning deserves every bit of goodness he can get."

It took me a minute to get what she was talking about. "Oh . . . yeah. Thanks! I'll tell him," I said, and hurried to the stairs, but she stepped outside her shop and grabbed my arm, the worried look back on her face.

"Wait a minute, honey," she said. "The cops were here looking for you early this morning when I came in. They didn't say what they wanted. They asked when you were going to be in, and I told them I didn't know. I called you at home to warn you, but you'd already left. Is everything okay?"

My stomach dropped. "I don't know, Wyvetta."

"You want to talk about it?"

"Not now."

"They're coming back. The young one was a right snotty little bastard. They said you have their cards and for you to call them when you got here or there would be trouble. If they ask you why you didn't call, just tell them you didn't get the message. Say the woman who owns the Biscuit is loon-crazy and don't remember nothing nobody tells her, okay?"

I smiled despite my feelings. "Thanks, Wyvetta."

"One more thing, Tamara. Mrs. Nellie Barnes just went upstairs, and she's waiting outside your door. I told her she could wait down here, but she looked upset, like she had something serious on her mind, so I let her go on up."

I shook my head. "This is all I need."

Wyvetta hugged me, and I could feel her strength through her nylon uniform. "I'm happy you got some good loving last night, baby. You gonna need it today. You want me to call Larry for you and tell him to come over here?"

"No," I said quickly. "I'll call him later, when I find out what's going on."

"Stop by here later and let's get some dinner. My treat."

I could hear Barnes's wife pacing outside my office as I climbed the stairs, so I took my own sweet time. I wondered what she wanted, but I was more concerned with the cops than her; I knew what they did.

"Good morning, Mrs. Barnes. Wyvetta Green told me you were waiting for me. Please come in and sit down," I said as graciously as I could, as I opened the door and stood back so she could enter.

Wyvetta had it right about the agitation. When she got inside, she paced back and forth in front of my desk, shaking her head as if listening to directions from a haint. Her summery pink dress looked like she'd slept in it, and her short black hair peeked like a bird's nest from beneath a wrinkled scarf. She wore sandals, a poor choice; the chipped nail polish on her toes said she should have taken Wyvetta up on her offer. An hour with Maydell would have done the woman a world of good.

"Please have a seat, Mrs. Barnes. Could I make you some tea or coffee?" She shook her head and, gaze fixed on the floor, continued to pace. "Please, ma'am," I said, and she glanced up at me as if just remembering she was in my office, but finally sat down.

"What can I do for you this morning?" I said after a decent pause.

"I'm sorry to trouble you, Ms. Hayle, but I'm worried about my family—my husband and my son. I haven't seen either of them since Wednesday morning. Troy disappears like this, and I know he'll probably show up sooner or later. It's something he's done since he came home from the war—leaving home, taking long rides, trying to forget what he saw—but Treyman . . . This isn't like Treyman."

"Have you called the police?"

She shook her head. "I don't want to get them involved yet. Treyman can't afford the publicity. He's involved in a very sensitive, very secretive negotiation about some real estate here in town, and it would be bad for people to know that he's missing. If I haven't heard from him by tonight . . ." She pleaded with her eyes. "Do you know anything about where he could be? Anything?"

"I'm sorry, but I really don't."

"He told me he was coming to see you that morning. His office manager was sick, so I'm not sure what time he got back to his office."

"He left here around eleven, if that's helpful," I said, not sure what to make of her. My first impression had been of a placid suburbanite in drab white linen. Thanks to her nasty husband and ashtray-throwing son, that meeting was now a painful blur. This new Nellie Barnes, stepping and fretting like a woman out the crazy house, was making me nervous.

"I don't know." She shook her head again. "He works late on Wednesdays, and he's usually home by midnight, but he didn't come home that night. There was a call at ten thirty, and I think it was him. I pray it was him, but I'm not sure. I'd taken an Ambien and was drifting off to sleep. I didn't bother to get it, and there was no message."

"You don't have caller ID?"

She nodded that she did. "His cell phone came up, but he never uses it except when he travels. Never from the office. Somebody else could have gotten his cell and used it."

"And you were home all day yesterday and today?"

"No. Well, I was on an early train to visit my mother yesterday morning, and I spent most of Thursday with her. I was sure I'd hear from him again, and when I got home, he wasn't there, and neither was my son, and I panicked."

"Maybe you simply missed him," I suggested. "He may have called you from his cell at an airport, telling you he had an emergency meeting somewhere about those sensitive negotiations you mentioned and didn't bother to leave a message, got involved in the meeting, and missed you again. Does he have your mother's telephone number?"

She looked anxious for a moment, then relieved. "Actually, he may not. Mother had it changed recently, and she's not sure how to retrieve messages."

"My bet is you've simply missed each other. Did you stop by his office today?"

"Not yet. I wanted to talk to you before I spoke to his manager. I don't want him to suspect there's any problem. He's not the nicest man in the world."

"I'm sure your husband is fine," I said. "No news is good news, as they say."

She smiled slightly, agreeing, and gave a sigh of relief. "You're probably right. Do you think I could have a cup of that tea you mentioned earlier?"

My day was clear, and I figured any time I spent comforting Barnes's wife was covered by that grand he'd given me, so I turned on my electric teakettle, got out my best mugs, and settled back to keep her company.

"Could you tell me what the two of you spoke about when you saw him on Wednesday morning?" She daintily tore open a packet of Splenda and stirred it into her tea.

"Actually, our meeting was quite brief," I said. "We had a rather . . . well, heated disagreement, and we didn't part on good terms. We decided there was no longer any need for me to be involved in the case."

She put down her tea, obviously disturbed. "Treyman can be difficult, but why did he fire you when the baby is still missing?"

"He didn't fire me; I quit. And I did locate the child and the woman who had her. Your husband was scheduled to meet with her. I'm really not sure what happened after that."

She gave me a wide-eyed stare that made me uneasy. "Then you found the child, and you told him. Why didn't he tell me?"

"I'm sorry, but I simply don't know. I wish I could give you more information, but I'm not . . . well, I'm not involved in your case any-more."

She stood up for a moment, and I thought she was going to leave, but she sat back down. "But my son, Troy. Did my husband mention him at all in any of your conversations?"

I recalled Barnes's comments about his kid and decided it was best to spare her.

"I'm afraid not. I haven't heard from or seen your son since that day in the office."

She shifted her gaze to her mug of tea. "You must have a very poor opinion of my family—of me, my husband, and son."

Got that right, I thought, but said, "No, I don't form opinions in my line of work. They usually turn out to be wrong."

"Do you have a husband, a son, by any chance?"

"Have a son, had a husband. We're divorced."

"How old is your son?"

"Teenager now."

"Does he get along with his father?"

"Now he does."

"It's hard for sons and fathers to get along sometimes. They can hold things against each other. Things that should be forgotten. But all a son really wants to do is please his father, live up to his father's ex-pectations, make his father proud of him."

"Yes, sometimes they do," I said, remembering the years before Jamal had made peace with DeWayne. For most of his childhood, he had blamed his father for the deaths of his half brothers. Finally, he'd been able to forgive him. At least for now. Did he still harbor resent-ment toward DeWayne or to me?

"My son loves his father deeply, but he also blames him for certain things."

"What things?"

She studied me for a moment, probably considering how much she wanted to tell me. I wanted to hear it, so I leaned toward her eager to listen.

"My husband is a good man. He wasn't always, but he is now. He was involved . . . well, in some bad things once. Unsavory things. But he's changed. He loves me; he takes care of me. I have certain . . . problems, Ms. Hayle.

"Sometimes the world gets very blue, and I'm unable to recover quickly. Sometimes things are fine. But I need to take my pills to get things balanced, put things in focus." She was embarrassed when she said it and wouldn't look me in the eye.

So the illness that Treyman Barnes had described was emo-tional rather than physical, maybe a form of depression, similar to what afflicted Jake's wife, Phyllis. She had been hospitalized for it, and I wondered if Nellie Barnes had spent time away from her family, too.

"I went through a particularly bad period while Troy was in Iraq."

"That's enough to send any mother through a particularly bad period," I said. I didn't want to imagine the torment I'd go through if Jamal went to war.

"I was better when he came back, but I was still sad. My son suffered . . . still suffers from what they call PTSD, post-traumatic stress disorder. Uncontrolled fear, raging anger. The say one in six men coming back have it. My son's in treatment for it now, and he's getting better, day by day, I can see it.

"My son blames Treyman for my moods, and maybe it did start with my anger toward him. Treyman thought that having Troy's baby live with us, helping my son raise her, might help us both. Having someone to spoil, raise a child again, I know it would bring joy to my life."

"That's an awful lot to put on a child," I said, and thought, *Better off with a cat*.

"I have a lot of love to give—we all do—and having her would make my son whole again."

I nodded as if I agreed but had my reservations. Children can't save a person's life, any more than an adult can. The only person who can save your life is you.

"What is your son like?" I asked, wondering if she really knew. How much does any woman really know about her son? If somebody had told me that Jamal would climb out of his bedroom window into crazy Lilah Love's rented car for a trip to Atlantic City, I would have thought they were smoking crack.

"This war, the senseless brutality of it, brought out a violence that I didn't know Troy had within him. But he has a good soul. He always has, especially as a little boy. I know it's still there. It has to be.

"I love my son, but to kill another person, even in war, takes away something. He's slowly reclaiming what he lost. Bit by bit."

"Your husband mentioned he was in the special forces."

"He never told us exactly what he did, but he is not who he was."

Damned fool was in them special forces. Trained killer was what he was. That's what he told me anyway. Trained killer. What the hell do I need with a trained killer?

Lilah's words came back.

"Troy is trying to get away from his past, the same as my husband," Nellie Barnes said, snatching my thoughts away from Lilah and back to her.

"And your husband's past?"

"The less I say about that, the better," she said with a firmness that surprised me. "He's a different man now. A good man, although some people refuse to believe it."

"Did you know that Lilah Love was dead?"

"Lilah Love?" She gave me a blank look.

Was it possible that she didn't know who Lilah was? How much in the dark had he kept her?

"The woman who was married to your son. The mother of your grandchild," I said.

"That was her name?"

"Yes," I said. *Was she putting me on?*

"The only thing that Treyman ever referred to her as was 'that little tramp,' and my son never mentioned her at all. He would just say 'the woman I was married to.' Talking about her seemed to upset him, so I never brought her up. They weren't together very long. How did she die?"

"And you didn't push it?" I asked, amazed.

"No."

"Why not?"

She paused for a moment, finally looking me in the eye. "Because I didn't want to know. I didn't want to know what nobody wanted to tell me. You didn't answer my question. How did she die?"

"Murdered," I said. "And very cruelly. Sadistically. Larynx smashed straight through to her spine. Body left to rot in the trunk of a rented car." The brutal words were spoken casually but were deliberately chosen because I wanted to see her reaction.

I didn't know what her quick, sharp intake of breath meant or why her hand flew to cover her mouth like it had that day in the office. Was it shock at hearing about a woman's murder or something else entirely, something she suddenly remembered?

"Do they have any idea who could have done it?" She recovered quickly.

"Yeah, they're pretty sure," I said, watching her closely because I knew what she must be thinking, what I would be thinking if I were in her shoes—about a damaged son with a short temper, a stolen baby, a woman whose name he couldn't say.

"My husband is a good man," she said out of nowhere, and I knew then it wasn't her son she was worried about.

"I'm sure he is."

So maybe Basil, rarely wrong about criminal minds because he had one himself, had gotten it wrong. Maybe I'd been right, that Treyman Barnes was mixed up in this mess. Or maybe they both were, father and son. Barnes getting Turk to kill Lilah and his son protecting his father by killing Turk. That was one way a troubled son could earn his distant father's love and respect. They could be out of the country by now, planning to send for Nellie later. But then why had Barnes come to my office looking for Baby Dal? How was Thelma Lee involved?

But there was no need to share any of these thoughts with Nellie Barnes. She carried on about her good-hearted son and "good man" of a husband and how much he loved her and where they had gone on their honeymoon and cruise last winter, and I sat there, sipping tea and watched her talk, wondering just how much information she didn't want to know that she'd tucked away. Wyvetta's name for her, Know-Nothing Nellie, had a heartbreaking resonance now.

Yet I felt a sense of relief.

"If I hear from either of them, you'll be the first to know," I said as I bid her goodbye.

"You're a good woman, Tamara Hayle," she said, and I hoped she'd still feel that way when she found out I'd tossed my red-meat suspicions about her family into the waiting jaws of the hungry cops.

I did some research on an upcoming case for the next couple of hours, then went to dinner with Wyvetta, sneaking out the back door like schoolkids and into her car in case any cops were around. Sitting across from her in our favorite Chinese restaurant, I got mad again when I thought of what Larry had said about her and Earl, and when she asked about him, all grins and expectations, it was all I could do not to share my real thoughts.

She didn't ask about what was going on in my life, and I didn't tell her. Better to share it over that bottle of bourbon when everything was over. She dropped me off in the back of our building so I could pick up some things in my office before I headed home. It was going on ten, and when I heard the knock on the door, I opened it quickly, assuming it was Wyvetta. It was the two cops again, looking tired and surly. They were dressed as they were before, same suits and ill-fitting jackets, but the young one had a day or two growth of beard that gave him a sinister edge.

"Hello again, Ms. Hayle. I'm Detective Coates, and this is Detective Ransom. May we come in?" asked the veteran.

"Of course," I said, standing back. No use acting like I had something to hide. But the glint in the rookie's eyes made me nervous.

"Monday," the rookie said.

"I beg your pardon?"

"Monday we want to talk to your son. There have been some . . . well, some new developments. He's a minor, but he's a possible witness to a violent crime, so we can't put it off any longer," said the veteran.

"If you think my son is somehow involved in Lilah Love's death, you're wrong, and as for anything else, he's been out of—"

"We know where he is, and we'll pick him up if you don't bring him to us. He's a material witness," the young one said, cutting me off.

"He didn't witness a damn thing," I said. But I knew it didn't matter. The police could hold a material witness almost as long as they wanted to. There were few protections against it.

"We'll be the ones who decide that. We don't want to go down there and pick him up unless we have to. It would be easier for the kid if you bring him in, make it casual like, don't put more on him than you need to," said the older cop.

"This whole thing stinks to high heaven, and every time we look up, the name *Hayle* seems to pops up," added the young one. His veteran partner shot him a warning glance.

"What are you talking about?" The skin on the back of my neck crawled down.

"Your son was the last person to see Lilah Love alive. As far as we can ascertain, you may have been the last person to meet with Treyman Barnes. His wife told us a little while ago that he was here with you the day before yesterday."

"Treyman Barnes! Are you telling me that Treyman Barnes is dead?!"

"Yeah, he's dead."

His words had an immediate, violent effect; I fell back against my desk like somebody had punched me. "He's dead? How could he be dead?" I hardly knew the man, and certainly hadn't liked him, yet even I was surprised by the intensity of my reaction. I could hardly breathe for a moment, maybe because of his wife, and what she must have felt when she found out. Or his son. If he hadn't had a hand in it. But mostly because my biggest fear was becoming a reality. The murderer was closing in and getting reckless. The cops, unimpressed by my response, stared at me blankly.

"Don't you listen to the news? It was on every station, first story. Big-time businessman found dead in the trunk of his car." The younger one smirked. "Somebody took him by surprise, probably handcuffed him, got him out of his office, and cut his throat, ear to ear, before they threw him in his fancy car," he said, as if he enjoyed telling me.

Execution-style. Cut his throat.

"But I just talked to his wife! She was just here!" I wailed, as if they would care.

"We know you were working for him. We know you had a heated disagreement, and we'll find out the rest," said the veteran.

"Have you talked to his son, to Troy Barnes? He had reason to want both Lilah and his father dead. He may have had something to do with Turk Orlando's death, too!" I said, pouring out everything I knew.

They glanced at each other again, then back at me. "Turk Orlando?" asked the rookie.

"The guy who was found in that motel, same MO."

"How do you know about Turk Orlando and how he was killed? The details haven't been released yet," said the veteran.

"Just how much do you know?" the young one demanded.

"Nothing," I said miserably. "I'm not going to say anything else without a lawyer present. I don't know anything!"

The veteran sighed, long and wearily, and said, "Look, I'm going to cut you some slack because I knew your brother, and I know you were in law enforcement a while back. But you'd better meet us at the precinct with your son and that lawyer first thing on Monday morning, you got it?"

"And don't leave town or we'll pick your kid up at his daddy's place," the young one added.

The veteran laid two cards on the edge of my desk, and the two of them left without looking back.

FIFTEEN

Y CELL PHONE RANG as I was walking to my car, and when DeWayne's name flashed on the screen, I picked it up quick.

"Is he there yet? I don't know where the hell else he could be but with you," he said before I could answer.

I stopped dead in my tracks, right where I stood.

"Did you hear me? Did Jamal get there yet? He's probably headed to—"

"Are you telling me that Jamal's not with you?"

"That's what I said."

"I just talked to him yesterday. Yesterday he said—"

"Today ain't yesterday, Tamara, and he ain't here today. I figured he's probably headed up to you. He said something about going home. I—" DeWayne couldn't finish because I was screaming at him, my fear and rage combining in a wail that came straight from my gut.

"Now, calm down, Tammy. The boy—"

"There's been another killing! The killer might be looking for

Jamal! The cops want Jamal here on Monday morning, so they'll be looking for him, too! They might even have him now, for all we know! How could you let this happen again? How could you let this happen?" My words rolled out in a tirade that left me breathless.

"Don't blame me. I got home this evening, and his bag was gone. I—"

"You stupid son of a bitch!" I spit out. "You careless, irresponsible, *stupid* son of a bitch!"

"No need to get nasty, now. This is as much your fault as it is mine. Who introduced him to the bitch in the first place? Who exposes him to lowlifes every day of the week? Who spoils the boy to the point where he don't know shit?" His accusations, shouted fast and loud, knocked my legs from under me, and I sat down on the curb, unable to speak. Everything had come apart. Every bit of peace I'd felt. Jamal's voice came back, mocking me.

I'm fine. Hey, Mom. Take a deep breath. Relax. Okay?

But he wasn't fine. I knew it now, and I should have known it then.

"Tamara, you still there?" asked DeWayne cautiously.

"Did he leave a note? Did he give any hint where he was going?" It did no good to scream at the fool or for him to scream at me. It just made things worse.

"He said something last night about being worried about *you* and wanting to get home. Said he didn't want to wait until Sunday. They still ain't found that killer yet? What you mean the cops want to see him on Monday?"

"They want me to bring him in so he has to be home by then."

Neither of us spoke. I could hear DeWayne breathing heavy on the line, as if he was trying to catch his breath. I knew he was as worried as me.

"Tamara, I'll find him, I promise," he said after a while, his voice low and earnest.

"Your promises don't mean shit to me, DeWayne Curtis, you know that."

"I promise on the memory of my boys, Tamara, I promise on that." He said it like a kid does, promising the world with a cross-my-heart-and-hope-to-die, but I knew that the memory of his sons, murdered because of his recklessness, was the only decent thing DeWayne had left; it was all he had to offer. "There's a bus leaving for Newark from Atlantic City around midnight. He probably made his way over there to catch that one. I'm going to drive over to the bus station and see if he's there. You go on home, and I'll call you from the station, okay?"

"Okay," I said after a while, because there was nothing else I could do.

I ran to my car thinking of nothing but my son, even the cops a memory. My car door wasn't locked, and I realized I'd forgotten to turn on the alarm system. Big mistake in this neighborhood. A few years back, Newark was known as the carjacking capital of the world. I was damn lucky my little red VW was still here.

I climbed in, put the key in the ignition, then realized I'd left the cops' cards on my desk. Worrying about Jamal had shaken their names right out of my head. I'd need those cards. After I'd checked in with DeWayne, I'd try to get Jake again and ask him what to do. He'd need to know their names. I tried the door to get out, and when the thing jammed, I cursed out loud. The cops had left a card when they came to my house. Maybe it was somewhere in the house. I didn't feel like messing with this door now. But as I turned the key in the ignition, someone hit me hard against the back of my head.

"Don't turn around," said the man behind me, his voice mean and cruel. "I want what is mine. Just drive and don't turn around."

"Troy Barnes," I said. Who else could it be?

I tried the door again for the hell of it, then realized even as I did that there was no use doing it. He wouldn't let me out. He must have jammed something on the way into my car. I put my hands back on the wheel.

"I need to go home, Mr. Barnes," I said without thinking. "Please let me—" I stopped short. If he was the killer, I needed to be as far away from home as I could get.

"What?" His voice was vague, with no tone, and I backtracked fast.

"Why did you break into my car?" I said, as if it mattered.

"Drive. No main streets. Cops are looking for me. Backstreets. Drive slow."

"Why did you break into my car?"

"Just drive," he said again. "Just drive around, slowly in a circle. I got to think." He was scared, I could hear that, but not as scared as me.

Wherever he wanted to take me, I was willing to go—as long as it wasn't home. I drove for the next twenty minutes. Down one street, up the next. Listening to every sound that he made, trying to figure out his moods. He sat straight as a soldier, and that scared me, too. I studied his face in my rearview mirror—eyes as haunted as they'd been the first time I saw him, homely face unshaven and mournful. I thought about the knife he surely had and about Turk Orlando and his father, Treyman Barnes. And then about Lilah Love and what she must have thrown in his face to set him off.

I got me a real man now. And them arms ain't the only place Turk's got muscles, if you know what I mean.

Could those or ones like it have been her final words to him, the ones that put his fist through her throat? He would have had to kill Turk then, too, because she'd told him whom she was meeting—the man with muscles everywhere. But why his father? I remembered Nellie Barnes's words about her boy and how all he wanted to do was live up to his father's expectations, make his father proud. Had he murdered his own father? Had he lost his temper, lost control of every decent thing he had in him? I'd read men had to do that when they killed in wars. Killing was killing, and sometimes a man couldn't stop.

Maybe his father had become the enemy. He'd sounded like one in his office that day. A father's expectations could be a double-edged sword, driving a son to success or making him crazy if he couldn't meet them. What had they done to Troy Barnes?

"What do you want from me?" I asked him, keeping my voice calm, cautious.

"I want my little girl."

"I don't have her."

"My father said you would know where she is."

"Your father is dead," I said.

Silence.

"You knew that, right? I'm not telling you something you didn't already know?" I was pushing it, but I didn't give a damn. I slowed the car, gave myself time to think, wonder what he was going to do. Should I hit something to throw him off balance? But he would kill me sure as I was sitting here. If he'd killed Lilah, if he'd killed Turk. His face caught the light that streamed in from the streetlights, and what I saw surprised me. He had covered his face with his hands and was crying hard and silently into them. His body shook with the sobs. Was it grief or remorse? I played it for all I could.

"The cops think you might have killed him," I said, exaggerating. Hell, the cops thought I might have killed him, too.

"You think I give a fuck what the cops think?"

"You'd better give a fuck!"

"Shut up!"

"Where were you anyway? They're going to ask you that. Where were you when he died?"

"None of your goddamn business!"

"You know how he died, don't you? Somebody slashed his throat, threw him in the trunk of his car, the same way *somebody* did your ex-wife!"

"Shut the fuck up! I didn't kill him. I didn't!"

"Where were you, then? Where? They're going to ask you that, you know that? The cops are going to ask you that."

I glanced in the rearview mirror at him. His hand was over his eyes as if he didn't want to see. *Remorse or grief?* I asked myself again.

"I was feeling down on Tuesday night. I went to the hospital, the VA hospital, and checked myself in for a few days. That's what they tell you to do. He was my dad. I loved him; why would I kill him?" He spoke in a hoarse whisper, his voice broken. I pushed him further.

"You tell me. You didn't seem to love him that much in the office that day, when you threw the ashtray at him. When you scared everybody including your mother half to death."

"I didn't throw it at him. I was mad, that was all. I was just fucking mad."

"You get mad like that often, don't you? Mad enough to kill somebody, slash somebody's throat?"

"Just fucking drive," he said, and I did, around and around and around the same goddamn six blocks. How many times had I driven down these streets? More times than I could remember, yet it was as if I'd never seen anything before: The CVS on the corner where I bought cheap makeup. The tacky little deli with its tasteless, weak coffee. China Wing, where Wyvetta and I had just shared shrimp egg foo young and peppered steak. Fear had turned everything unfamiliar. "All I want is my little girl," he muttered from the back, breaking the silence. "That's all I want, and I'll kill anybody who tries to stop me from getting her."

He settled back in his seat then, tired it seemed from the words he'd uttered. I tried my door again, cursed to myself. No way would it open. Those last words about killing scared me, but I didn't want him to know it. I waited ten minutes before speaking again.

"Do you have any idea who could have done it, killed your dad?"

My tone was conciliatory, the good cop, understanding and wise. But I wasn't sure about the man, and I sure as hell didn't trust him.

He dropped his head down to his chest and shook it hard. I thought maybe he might be telling me the truth. But that didn't say squat about Lilah or Turk.

It was nobody's business what she did with what was hers.

Had she decided to keep the baby, figuring she could milk his family for as long as she needed to?

"Your mom came by to see me today," I said, when he didn't answer. "She's a nice lady, loves you very much, believes in you, thinks you're going to get better. How come you didn't bother to tell her the name of the mother of your baby, and that she was dead?"

"It didn't matter one way or the other."

"Because Lilah was dead?"

He waited a few minutes before he answered. "Because I didn't mean shit to Lilah Love, and neither did my kid. I didn't want to say her name any more than I had to."

"Your father said she got what was coming to her. Do you think he was right?" I threw it out, taking a chance, studying his face in the mirror, waiting for him to speak, and when he did, his voice was surprisingly tender but matter-of-fact.

"I loved Lilah once, and she was the mother of my baby. She didn't deserve to die like that. Nobody does." I wondered again if he was trying to fool me. But I'd seen enough killers in my day to know that they always found a way to brag about what they did. They had to make you see their point, appreciate the desperation that had brought out the killer in them, and they usually explained it to you right about the time they were trying to take your life.

But he wasn't bragging. His words were sad, regretful; surprisingly, they softened the tension between us.

"You know a girl named Maydell?" I said after a while.

She'd come to me suddenly, with her easygoing, lazy style. Despite what Wyvetta said, Maydell had a good sense of people, keen enough to spot a good tipper—or a *real* gangster. Her name brought a trace of a smile and an easing of the taut line across his forehead.

"Maydell Washington?"

"Said she knew you in high school."

"Yeah, I know Maydell. How's she doing?" he seemed genuinely interested, a good sign. I made a note to give the girl a big tip if I got out of this car alive.

"Fine. Called you a true-blue war hero. True-blue was what she said. What do you think about that?"

There was a glimmer of light in those sad eyes, and I could glimpse for a moment what he must have looked like as a little boy, the good soul his mother said he was.

"Maydell always saw the best in everybody, even if they didn't deserve it. I should have married her instead of Lilah."

"You would have been a damn sight better off."

"Thanks for telling me about Maydell. If you see her again, tell her I said hi, okay?"

"Yeah, sure. So was she telling the truth? Are you a true-blue war hero?" I'd heard a lot of strange stuff about this kid and didn't know what to believe. His father said he was a nutcase, and Lilah called him a trained killer. But he was true-blue to Maydell Washington, whatever that meant, and his mama loved him like mamas do.

"What branch were you in?" I asked him.

"Special forces."

"What did you do?"

"Nothing I want to talk about."

"Bad dreams?"

"Yeah, sure, I get them."

There was nothing for a while, and that made me nervous. I didn't want to lose our connection, as tenuous as it was. "Hey, Troy, you still with me?"

"About people that died. Kids sometimes. Kids I saw blown apart. Women. I talk to people now. Guys at the center who spent some time in the Gulf or Nam. Guys who have been through the same as me. I wanted to, you know, to kill myself when I got back."

I thought about my brother and didn't say anything for a while.

"Are you getting some help?"

"Yeah. At the VA. The nightmares have stopped. I can control my anger more than before, but every now and then, it comes out like it did at my dad over bullshit. I don't sleep with a .45 underneath my pillow anymore, if that's what you want to know. But I need to get my kid back. I need to hold her and know she's okay. She and my mom, you know, are all . . ."

He stopped then, not wanting to finish it, not needing to.

"My father didn't give a shit about me. I disappointed him from the day I was born. My mom was the person who was important to me. She was the center of my life. My dad, well, I needed him, and he was never there, didn't want to be."

I thought about my own son then, and dread cut through me. When I glanced back, he was weeping.

My phone rang, and Troy Barnes jumped. His nerves were tight, and that worried me.

"It might be my boy. Can I answer it?" I asked his permission, trusting him because of what he'd said about his mama and because I had no other choice. He nodded that I could. It wasn't Jamal but De-

Wayne. "I've got him" was all he said, and my eyes filled with tears of relief.

We drove for another ten minutes, the silence between us uneasy but not hostile.

"Troy?" I said his name gently, breaking the tension.

"Yeah."

"How you doing back there?"

"Okay. I wasn't going to hurt you, even if you didn't help me," he said.

"I know," I said, like I believed him. "Can I ask you something?"

"Sure."

"What makes you think I know where your baby is?" I glanced at the rearview mirror, and his eyes met mine.

"My dad said he traced the number that flashed on his phone when Lilah's sister called him Wednesday night. The call came from your house. The girl said she knew where the baby was and wanted us to have her. My dad said he'd bet his life that you knew where my daughter was."

"He probably did," I said.

"Yeah, he did."

Another silence, easier this time.

"All I want is my kid, that's all. I've never seen her. Just that picture Lilah sent me. Lilah's dead, my dad is gone, there's nobody else I can turn to. Will you help me get her back?"

I guess it was because God had smiled on me tonight. My son was safe, at least until Monday—and I owed Him a good deed for that. And maybe because that cute little baby with her pretty dimples had touched my heart. I knew I had to help this boy. I didn't think he was the killer, but whoever had murdered those three people was still out there, and my son wouldn't be safe until I knew who it was. I had to find out what Thelma Lee knew. I pulled over to the side of the road and took out my cell.

"You calling the cops," Troy said, all the fight gone out of him.

"No. Thelma Lee Sweets, Lilah's sister."

"I just want to hold my baby once, and know she's real. I can take anything after that. Do you think Thelma Lee still has her?"

"She might."

It was going on nine. Late, but Thelma Lee was probably home by now. Where else did she have to go?

So Troy Barnes fixed the door to my car as best he could, then climbed into the passenger seat, and I drove fast to Jersey City to look for Thelma Lee "Trinity" Sweets and find out what she knew.

SIXTEEN

"WHAT IS SHE LIKE, THELMA LEE?" Troy Barnes asked on the way to Jersey City. He sounded worried, probably scared he'd run into another Lilah Love.

"She's a teenager. Likes to call herself Trinity after that woman in the movie. Seems like a nice kid, but you can't always tell about people. They're hard to read sometimes."

"You read me."

"You? True-blue?" I quoted Maydell, which made him smile. After our rocky first encounter, the ride over had been almost pleasant. He did most of the talking—about things that he'd seen in the war and the guilt and anger that darkened his life. He wept again when he talked about his friends—the dead ones he'd left in pieces on the streets of Fallujah, and the ones who were barely making it now. The war had changed him forever, he said, and everyone said he would be better because of it, but he didn't believe them. Mostly, though, he talked about his daughter, and what it had meant to him when Lilah sent him her picture. He described how he'd shown it to everybody in his squad and worn it pinned to his undershirt next to his heart. It had kept him alive, he said, just thinking about her and fantasizing about his life with her when he finally came home. He imagined her as a toddler, a schoolgirl, a teenager. He saw visions of her in her prom dress and on the way to her wedding. He knew the words he would say when he gave her away. Nothing else mattered but her. Nothing else in his life. Baby Dal was his link to the present and future, his tie with all that was good.

He suspected all along that Lilah wouldn't stay with him, and when the letter came telling him she was leaving, it wasn't a surprise. He asked me where I knew her from, and I told him the truth, that she'd been a good kid when I met her in Jamaica, but something had changed her, and I wasn't sure what.

"Maybe she went through a war, too," he said. "A personal one that she kept to herself."

"Maybe she did," I said.

He was quiet for a while, then said he had to try to understand who she was so he could explain her to their daughter one day, and I nodded that he should. People give the best part of themselves to their kids, I said, thinking about DeWayne Curtis and Jamal. And Lilah had given the best of herself to her child. When the time came to explain, he'd know what to say.

"Do you know why Thelma Lee took the baby?" he asked.

"She told me that Lilah wasn't a good mother," I said. He nodded as if he understood, then sighed like the weight of the world had fallen on him. "But the baby's okay," I added quickly to reassure him.

"You saw her, then?" he asked, eyes anxious.

"No, but Thelma Lee and her aunt seem to love her very much, and I'm sure they are taking the best care of her that they can."

"Lilah tried to get money from my father. He offered to pay her, but she said it wasn't enough. When we didn't hear from her again, he hired you to find the baby. I'm sorry Lilah is dead, but I don't know if I can forgive her like you said I should," he said.

"Everything in life takes time," I said, because everything did. It took me years to forgive my parents for their joke of a marriage, and I have never gotten over my mother's cruelty. As for Johnny, my love for him has been unconditional even in death, but I am still angry. I wondered how much Jamal would need to forgive.

"Do you think my daughter is in any danger, from the person who killed my father?"

"I doubt it," I said quickly, but I wasn't as sure about Thelma Lee as I was of this man sitting beside me. There was still a trace of doubt. I didn't think she'd hurt the baby, but she could have had it in for Lilah and Turk. As for Treyman Barnes, I couldn't see her killing him like he had been killed. But there was enough of the cop in me to keep a few doubts simmering until everything was clear, and it was murky. I didn't know the how, why, where, or when of it yet, and that worried me. I did know I needed to convince Thelma Lee to talk to the police with me on Monday morning. She had been at the murder scene before and after Turk Orlando was killed, and she probably knew more about the murder than she thought she did, which put her in danger. She was a minor, and Jake could look out for her interests, too. If she refused to come, that would tell me something, too.

We pulled up in front of Sweet Thing's place around ten. The windows of Manhattan sparkled in the distance, and the full moon bathed the old house in flattering light, making it nearly the equal of its neighbors.

"She lives here?" Troy Barnes asked.

"Her aunt does."

"Big place," he said, getting out of the car.

"Let me go first. They know me."

"No way! I've waited too long."

He followed me onto the porch, the broken boards threatening to give way with each step. It was dark and took me a while to find the doorbell. I rang it once, then knocked as hard as I could. I had come full circle. It was hard to believe that it hadn't been a week since my first visit here.

"It's Tamara Hayle. I know you're in there, Thelma Lee Sweets. Open the door. I need to talk to you. Now!"

A light went on in the second floor and a few moments later in the living room. Somebody fumbled with the lock, then Sweet Thing stood in front of me, babe in arms. The baby gurgled, and all eyes turned to her.

"Baby Dal?" I asked.

"I call her Dolly," said Sweet Thing. "I don't believe in calling a child after a food I ain't et."

The baby was dressed all in pink, possibly the only color her mother had bothered to buy, and grinned at me, then at her father as if she knew who he was. She had grown since the photo Lilah showed me in the office. She was plumper and prettier, but her face was still framed in that black halo that looked as soft as spun cotton. She giggled, dimples peeking out from chubby cheeks, and hid her head in Sweet Thing's ample breast.

"This is Troy Barnes . . . Lily's ex-husband. The child's father," I said, with a nod toward Troy. Sweet Thing glanced at me, then at Troy Barnes, and put her arm protectively around the child. "Who you say you were?"

"The baby's father," I said.

"I ain't talking to you; I'm talking to him. Can't he speak for himself? If he can't speak for himself, he ain't going to hold this baby," she said, cutting her eyes at me.

"I'm Lilah's husband. Ex-husband. Baby Dal's father."

"Lilah? We called her Lily, after my baby sister. You didn't have nothing to do with naming this baby after that food, did you?" She pursed her lips in disgust.

"No," he said. "But that's her name, and it's going to stay that way. Can I hold her?"

"I don't know," said Sweet Thing, eyes narrowed.

"Please, ma'am, I've never held my child."

"How do I know you're really her daddy? How do I know that?"

"He's Treyman Barnes's son," I said, then thought better of it.

"You ain't like your father, are you?" Contempt replaced the curiosity that had been in her eyes.

"No. I never was, but my father's dead now," Troy said, and Sweet Thing turned to me, her eyes hard.

"When did he die? I ain't heard nothing about it."

"Very recently," I said.

"Somebody finally got him, huh?" she said. Her glance followed mine toward his son, and her face softened.

"I'm sorry for your loss, boy, I truly am," she said, "but he did a lot of people no good. He may have been a good daddy, but he was a dishonest son of a bitch as far as I'm concerned."

"He wasn't a good daddy either," Troy said. "But I loved him anyway."

"If you can find some love in your heart for a man like that, then you must have a very big heart. Here, take your baby and love her with all you got."

When Troy Barnes held his child for the first time, I knew that the look in his eyes would be with me forever—one of those memories I'd tuck away and summon whenever I needed to believe in good over evil, kindness over cruelty, or simply to smile. His eyes widened slightly as if in wonder, and then he closed them as he pulled her into his chest, rocking her back and forth as if he were in a special kind of ecstasy. I glanced at Sweet Thing and saw that there were tears in her eyes, too.

"Life do have a way of righting itself, don't it?" she said, and I nodded that it did.

"So what you doing knocking at my door at this time of night, Tamara Hayle?" she said, turning to me. "Where's my niece?"

"She isn't here?"

"No." She looked at me suspiciously. "Did you call to say you were coming? The phone ain't rung since Jimson left for work, and he didn't say nothing about nobody coming over. It's not like him to forget; he writes everything down for me. My feet hurt something fierce, and I can't be bothered getting to that damn phone."

"No, I haven't spoken to him. Is he around?" I should have known that he wasn't. I was struck again by how spirited this woman was as long as Jimson Weed, her lover and protector, was nowhere in sight. She could clearly take care of herself, and this baby, if she needed to.

"He works nights. Night watchman over at a building downtown. He'll be back in the morning."

She shrugged as if puzzled. "Come on in," she said, beckoning us into her home. Troy and I settled down on the couch in front of the TV. I thought about the first time I'd been here, the smell of burned toast and fried bacon coming from the kitchen, Jimson Weed hovering around Sweet Thing as if he owned her.

"Lily didn't say much about you when she dropped Dolly off. Tell me about yourself, boy." Sweet Thing turned to Troy.

"Not much to tell," Troy said. The baby began to fret, and Sweet Thing went into the kitchen and brought back a bottle.

"I was in the service. Iraq war. Came home. Trying to get over that," he said as the baby settled down. "What does she eat?"

"I got some formula from Costco day before yesterday. That will hold her for a while. Service, you say. What branch?"

"Army."

"Just like my sweet Jimson, when I met him," she said, her eyes clouding over with some emotion I couldn't read. "He came back so tore up, so violent, it took all I had to cure him. Every bit of patience I had I spent on him." She pulled a Marlboro out of the purple case on the coffee table, lit it, and inhaled hard. "Things never change, do they? That's what Jimson says, and I believe he's right."

I nodded, recalling what he'd said to me the day I met him about shit never going nowhere, just coming back. I wondered how often he'd told her that.

"He was in Nam?" asked Troy, his interest perking up as he looked up from the baby, who had fallen asleep on his shoulder.

"That's blood for you, ain't it?" Sweet Thing gave him an approving grin. "That child ain't seen you more than fifteen minutes, but she done fell asleep on your shoulder like she knew you all her life. She don't do that for just anybody. The minute Jimson picks her up, she cries."

"When did he go over?" asked Troy, still curious about Jimson Weed. His eyes had filled with compassion. I'd seen it before between men who had fought in Vietnam, and now young vets in this latest one. It was a bond they shared, men like Jimson Weed and Troy Barnes, and no one could know it unless they'd seen killing like they had. Unjust wars with no winner, my friend Annie would say. As if any war could ever be just.

"In '65, part of that first big wave. Came back decorated, too. Decorated hero, they told him."

"True-blue hero," Troy said to me with a slight, sad smile.

"True-blue hero or whatever else you want it call it," continued Sweet Thing. "But it didn't mean squat. Jimson couldn't find work, couldn't find nobody to help him. He stopped telling folks he even fought. Threw them medals right in the trash. Didn't mean nothing to him. Nothing did for the longest time."

"I couldn't find any meaning either. Not for a long time until now."

"Love will do that," Sweet Thing said.

"So how long have you-all been married?" The baby stirred slightly, then burped.

"Married? We ain't married. He's younger than me by ten years. I always did end up with young, good-looking men. You wouldn't know it now, but I was a looker in my day. Always did like young men."

I recalled Lilah's words about young and old men, but thought it best to keep them to myself.

"He came into my life two days after my sister was killed. Lily's mama. She was named Lily, too. He was my angel of light, that man, said it was his responsibility to take care of me, look after me, and he's done it for all these years."

"How did Lily die?" Troy asked.

"Murdered. In a den of sin. That's what Jimson used to call it. A den of sin. Lily bought this house right before she died. Bought it in 1979. Saved hard and bought it. Bought it for her daughters. Money right out her flesh. I ain't nothing but a tenant in it, as far as I'm concerned. I promised her I'd keep it safe for her kids, and their kids, too, so we'd always have some roots, always have a home. Right out her flesh, that's what this place is."

I glanced at Troy to see if he understood just how much flesh the house had cost his baby's grandmother, but he didn't take her literally. I recalled Basil's words about Treyman Barnes. *A filthy business* he'd called Barnes's youthful occupation. Funny when you thought about it: the "lofty" Barnes and "lowly" Sweets had more in common than one would think.

"She wanted to bring her daughters up nice, Lily did. Just like real little ladies," Sweet Thing continued. "And I done the best I could. Thelma Lee was just a baby when she died, and Lily—Lilah, as you call her—was older. I used to take care of them while their mama was at work. This house belongs to them—to Thelma Lee and that baby since her mother is gone.

"We came up hard, me and Lily. People nowadays don't know what tough times are. I didn't do right by her. I just didn't do right. I couldn't in those days.

"Things that happened to me down there in Mississippi, I ain't told nobody yet, don't nobody have a right to know," she said. Her eyes grew troubled, and sorrow shaded her face. I nodded because I understood. The Jim Crow South had been bad, but Mississippi was the worst. Black women raped, black men lynched, was as common as Mississippi mud, and nobody in power gave a damn. People ran from the South to save their lives. It wasn't that much different up north, but you couldn't be shot for not getting off the sidewalk to let a white man pass.

But there were still the memories. Race memories, my grandma called them. Up until the day she died, she warned me that white men could "ruin you." Sweet Thing probably had stories that hurt too much to tell and were best left unshared.

"I did the best I could do with what I had," she said. "I just hope she don't blame me much."

"Lily?" I called Lilah by her given name, but Sweet Thing said nothing.

Troy, more interested in his newfound baby than Sweet Thing's memories, didn't ask more questions after that. He did, however, call his mother and tell her where he was, and when he glanced at me, his eyes said he was ready to leave.

"You going to take that baby with you?" Sweet Thing asked as he began to gather her things.

"She's my daughter."

"A daughter is something you don't never throw away," she said, her gaze dropping to the floor.

"You don't have to worry about that!" Troy said.

"You going to bring her back to visit?" she pleaded with her voice and eyes.

"You're her family, same as me. My dad is dead. Lilah's dead. She doesn't have too much family left, does she? Me, you, my mom, Thelma Lee, that's it."

"Speaking of Thelma, why did you think she was with me when we came by tonight?" I asked Sweet Thing, recalling her earlier words. I'd almost forgotten the reason we'd come.

Sweet Thing shrugged. "Said she had to go to your house."

"My house? Why?"

"Said she was going back for something she'd left and to drop off something she'd taken. I don't know what the girl was talking about."

"How long ago did she leave?"

"She left with Jimson around nine o'clock, about an hour before you got here. He said he'd drop her off at your house and go to work from there."

I glanced at my watch. "It's late for her to be coming home by her-self."

"She might be waiting for you. I told her to call you, but she said she had to tell you in person."

"Did she say what?"

"No, just said you'd want to know."

"She's probably still at my house. I haven't been home yet," I said, and a chill crawled down my back, that sense I get when things aren't falling right. Troy Barnes glanced at me again, his baby asleep on his shoulder. It was time for him to take his daughter home.

But I didn't like leaving this vulnerable woman by herself. There had been too many killings already, and I didn't know the reasons yet.

"Why don't you come home with me?" I said. "Thelma's there, and you both can spend the night. I'll drive you back tomorrow."

"That's nice of you, Miss Hayle, but I don't think so," she said with a shy smile. "I'm going to stay right here. Jimson wouldn't like it if I left without telling him."

"Then don't tell him!"

"He'd know," she said, not looking me in the eye. There was a darkness to this love I hadn't seen.

"But you shouldn't be here by yourself," I said. She lit a cigarette, sucking the smoke in deep, reminding me of the day I met her.

"You talking about Lily?"

"And the others."

"Who else besides Lily and this boy's daddy?"

"Turk Orlando."

"The boy come over here with Lily?"

"Did you know he was dead?"

"I got to stay here and wait for Jimson. He'll be worried about me if he don't find me here," she said, staring at the smoke from her cigarette and avoiding my question.

"Aren't you afraid?"

"Jimson Weed will be here soon."

"He's not a young man."

"He's stronger than he look."

"To tell the truth, I could use your company," I said.

"You scared?"

"A little," I admitted. "Three women together are always stronger than one."

"You think Thelma still over there?"

"Probably. I tried to call her earlier, but she didn't answer the phone. There are some dead spots in my house where cell phones don't work. She may not have picked up the signal."

"That's why I don't bother with the damn things half the time. What good is a phone if it don't work? But I'll ride over there with you if you want me to. Ain't no fun being scared."

"Thanks," I said, relieved.

So she threw a few overnight things for herself and Thelma Lee into a paper bag, and the four of us piled into my car—Sweet Thing with her black handbag on her lap in the passenger seat and Troy laden down with baby and supplies in the back. I was glad the night was finally over. Monday was coming soon enough.

I dropped Troy Barnes off at his mother's place—a big, sprawling mansion in a fancy gated neighborhood just ten minutes from where I live. Sweet Thing's eyes got big when she saw it.

"She got two big houses now, from her mama and her daddy. She's going to grow up to be a real little lady, just like my Lily would want. Don't forget me, Dolly," she whispered to the baby, kissing her gently so she wouldn't wake her.

I helped Troy unload the car but left before he opened the door to go inside. He and Nellie Barnes deserved privacy to celebrate their joy and cry their tears.

"Did Thelma Lee mention what she left at my place?" I asked Sweet Thing as I drove home.

"It must have been that bracelet. The one her mama left her."

"But she should have it by now," I said, more to myself than to Sweet Thing, who had closed her eyes and looked as if she were nodding off.

Every light in my house was on, which told me that Thelma had looked high and low for her bracelet. I left Sweet Thing asleep in the car and ran up the stairs and in through the front door.

"Thelma Lee!" I yelled out, then ran upstairs, searched, and ran back down calling her name, but the house was empty. I found a note on the kitchen table, neatly printed on a paper towel, the spare keys that I keep over the dryer in the basement laid on top of it.

Dear Miss Hayle,

It's me, Trinity Sweets, again. I was going to wait for you but changed my mind. It wasn't all that important. Here are the keys I took when I went to buy them donuts. Forgot I put them in my pocket. Sorry about that!!

I lost my charm bracelet, the only thing my mama left me. Except Aunt Edna's house, which my sister wanted to sell. But now she's gone, so I guess we get to keep it.

I looked everywhere for that bracelet, but it's not here. I must have lost it in the other place, where my mama's soul lives. Jimson said if I didn't find it here, he'd take me there to get it before he went to work.

Your friend,
Trinity Sweets (Thelma Lee)

Suddenly everything fell into place.

SEVENTEEN

GOT TO GET BACK SOMETHING *that belongs to me. Something important. Stolen property, you might say. It's mine, and I want it back.*

It was that grand old house Lilah had been talking about, the one bought with her mother's flesh. It was hers, and she would get the biggest, fastest buck she could for it. Selling Baby Dal was an afterthought.

"Thelma ain't in there?" Sweet Thing's voice was calm when I got back, but her eyes were filled with fear. "She must have gone back home. We must have just missed her. You can drop me off at the PATH train. I don't want you to have to go all the way—"

"She didn't go home, Miss Sweets." I gave her the note, and she read it quickly.

"What does it mean?"

"Just what it says."

"Call her to see where she is! Call her!"

I did, and there was no answer, which was no surprise. "Jimson Weed took her to the place where your sister died, Miss Sweets. He took her to find a bracelet he already had. I know because I gave it to him the day she lost it."

"But why would he do something like that?" she asked. I shrugged as if I didn't understand, although I did.

I know everything that affects you, baby. Everything.

He knew about every call she got. He feared anyone who kept him from controlling her. He protected her from people he deemed her enemies, which was everyone but him.

Sometimes I think he loves me more than is good for him. You ever have a man love you like that?

Did she know she was his prisoner?

I glanced at her now, head resting wearily against the window, eyes closed.

"Jimson wouldn't hurt that child. I know that. We're family, Miss Hayle. He forgot about that bracelet, that's what he did. He'll tell you that himself when I talk to him like I do."

I drove on without speaking, focusing on the road ahead as Edna Sweets, Jimson Weed's Sweet Thing, rambled and cried about her good man and how much he loved her. It was what she believed, so I let her have it for as long as I could. But not forever.

"Why did Lilah come back home?" I said after a while. We were close to the motel where he had taken her. She looked at me as if she didn't understand what I was saying.

"Lily's dead."

"She told you she was going to sell that house, didn't she? She told you she didn't care where you went or what you did, but it was her house to sell, and she was throwing you out. And he stood there, and he listened to her, didn't he? He knew how much you loved that place, what it meant to you and your sister, that you had nowhere else to go."

"Lily never was no good. She never was no good, but I loved her anyway, God help me, I loved her anyway, and He is punishing me for what I did to her, what I didn't do."

Who was she talking about? Lily or Lilah? Did she even know the difference?

"What didn't you do for Lily?"

"I didn't claim her."

"Lilah didn't give a damn about you, Miss Sweets, she told me that. She didn't love Thelma Lee, either. She just loved herself. You shouldn't blame yourself for her. Why should you claim her? She didn't claim you," I said, hoping to give the woman some peace, some resolution.

She looked at me then, and her eyes were filled with anguish. "I'm talking about *my* Lily, Miss Hayle. Lily Sweets was my only daughter, and I never told her nothing. I came up here from Mississippi, raised her like my sister, never told the truth to her or nobody else. You live a lie, and there's no end to it."

Her words stunned me; there was nothing I could say. I stole a look at Sweet Thing's face and saw the image of the woman in Thelma Lee's locket, the one as pretty as her Aunt Edna, except for the soft beige of her skin.

Things that happened to me down in Mississippi, I ain't told nobody yet, don't nobody have a right to know.

I understood then what I had seen in her eyes. She'd been "ruined" down there in Mississippi, so she'd brought her baby north, kept her shame to herself, found a new life for her and Lily. But nothing had turned out like it was supposed to.

"What happened to your Lily?" I asked, as gently as I could.

"Drugs," she said.

And who had supplied those drugs? I was pretty sure I knew.

Why had she told me this now? Could it have been holding Baby Dal, her great-grandchild, whose dimpled grin had brought her to the truth? Or the death of Lilah Love and the danger now confronting Thelma Lee. Did she know what I did now? Had she always known it?

It's easy to tell a stranger a truth that you're ashamed of, and it was pure chance that she had chosen me. We rode in silence then, her lost in her thoughts, me in mine. The time for words was over, so we gave the truth the quiet it deserved.

As we approached the motel, its harsh neon lights threw yellow rays into the dark car, illuminating her pretty skin and high cheekbones, and I saw her as he must have when he got home from the war. His beautiful woman. Miss Edna Sweets.

Shit don't never go nowhere. Just back to where it come from when you don't expect to see it.

The truth had come back for Edna Sweets, and it would come for him as well. I'd call the police before I confronted him. I knew now what he was capable of, and what he'd done. Lilah died because she was after that house, and Turk because she told him whom she was meeting the night she was killed. Jamal had overheard that conversation. I was just lucky he didn't know who my son was. He would have known or guessed where Thelma Lee and Turk would go that night.

It would be risky for him to leave her alive. But why had he killed Treyman Barnes? Had killing become a habit?

I glanced over at Sweet Thing, remembering how gently he had taken her hand that morning in my office.

"Miss Sweets?" Her eyes were fixed on the window, her fingers clasped in her lap; she was lost and broken.

"Miss Sweets, I'm going to go inside the motel to see if Jimson has Thelma in there, and I'm going to call the police and tell them what I know. Do you understand me?"

She glanced at me as if she didn't know me.

"I'll be back as soon as the police come. Stay here and wait for me, okay?"

Her head dropped to her chest.

I got out of the car and headed for the lobby. The place deserved its reputation. The walls were a shitty brown, and the lobby smelled like pee. The room was bare except for two scarred orange sofas that looked as if some deranged soul had taken a knife to them. A light-skinned man with muttonchops and a name tag that said "Herbert" sat behind the desk reading the sports section of *The Star-Ledger*.

"Rooms are twenty an hour, sixty for the night. Cash money," he said without looking up.

"I'm not here for a room. I'm looking for two people. A teenager and an older man in his sixties."

He put down his paper and stared at me. "You've got to be fucking kidding," he said.

"No, as a matter of fact, I'm not," I said, with a dignified lift of my head.

"Teenagers with old men? That's all who comes through here. What you want? White, white; black, black; male, male; female, male, female?" Disgusted, he went back to his paper.

"The teenager's name is Thelma Lee Sweets. She was here on Tuesday night; she was with that man who got his throat cut." That got his attention. He put the paper down.

"Who did you say you were?"

"I'm Tamara Hayle, a private investigator," I said, and handed him a card.

He glanced at it, then back at me. "Who sent you?"

"The girl's guardian. She's underage."

He went back to the paper. "I just came on duty, so I ain't seen nothing. Half the girls come in here are what you call underage. What she look like?"

"About sixteen, probably in black, hair pulled back, plump, pretty face—"

He looked up. "You talking about Trinity?"

"Yes! You know her?"

"Sure, everybody knows Trinity. Likes to go up there to 311 and sit on the bed. She'll sit in that damn room for an hour or so, then come back downstairs. Never touches nothing. Don't even use the bathroom.

"But she ain't here now. Never comes at night. Just in the afternoon, when hardly nobody is here. She says she don't like old men staring at her tits."

"Are you sure?"

"Well, sure, they stare. I told her ain't nothing she can do about it.

That girl acts like she's from a different planet sometimes. She's a good-looking girl, and men—"

"No, fool! Are you sure about her not being here?" I said without thinking.

"Who you calling a fool?" He poked his chest out belligerently.

"Sorry."

"Yeah, I'm sure. You got some wrong information, sweetheart. First of all, Trinity wouldn't be with a guy like that, dumb enough to get his throat cut. She's a nice kid, schoolgirl who likes to dress like a freak. She wouldn't be mixed up in something like that."

"What room was he killed in?"

"Three eleven." He looked confused for a moment, then shook his head. "That's Trinity's room all right. But she can't be there now because nobody is. We can't let nobody in there. The cops closed that room up. It's a crime scene. The whole damn floor is closed."

"She's here, I know it. And she's in trouble." I leaned toward him, my voice urgent. "Listen, you need to call the police right now and tell them to come quick because a girl's life is in danger."

"Don't you got a cell phone?"

"Yes, but I'm not sure if . . . well, I'd rather not . . . uh . . . talk to the police at this point. It would be better if you did."

He gave me a knowing smirk and went back to his paper.

"What the hell is wrong with you? Did you hear what I just said? Trinity is up there! She's with a man named Jimson Weed, who is a killer. He's the one who—"

The man slowly folded the newspaper in a neat square and placed it on the counter. "Where you think you at, the Hilton? You want me to call the goddamn police? Sure, I'll call the goddamn police. Watch me!"

He picked up the phone, dialed 911, then repeated what I'd just told him, giving the address of the motel and his number. With a triumphant grin, he placed the phone back on the hook.

"What did they say?" I asked.

"What do you think they said?"

"Are they coming?"

"Yeah, that's what they said. They said they were on their way, and they will be here . . . in an hour or two."

"But a man was murdered here on Tuesday night! Do they realize that? Did you tell them what I said?"

"Didn't you just hear me tell them?" He cocked his head and glared at me. "Now, you listen to me, lady. I call the goddamn cops at least five times a night about mess going on around here, and you know how long it takes them to come? Half the time, my shift is over when they stroll through the door. They don't give a shit about this place or anybody in it. As far as they're concerned, people who come in here deserve what they get."

"But you know Trinity! Why don't you—"

He looked at me contemptuously. "Yeah, I do know Trinity, and I know she didn't have nothing to do with that murder like you said, and I know she don't come here at this time of night because she's a good kid, and I know she ain't nowhere in this place. I called the cops for you, that's all I'm going to do, because the person I don't know is *you!* For all I know, you're just some nut come in here off the street, carrying on about some murder that ain't gonna happen. You got trouble with the police your own self. Why should I listen to you?"

"But—"

He glanced at my card. "I'll tell you what I'm gonna do, Miss Tamara Hayle Private Investigator. I'm going to give you the benefit of a doubt, since I'm a nice guy and want to finish my paper in peace. I'm going to let *you* look for whoever it is you're looking for, so you can get the hell out of my face. You want to look for some kid, be my guest." He tossed me a key ring filled with keys. "Half are empty anyway since that murder. But knock before you go in, and bring these back in fifteen minutes. Don't use the elevator; it's been broke all week."

I stood there a moment, too stunned and angry to move, then ran up to the second floor, found Room 211, listened at the door, and opened it.

"What the fuck?" A gray-haired white man, butt-naked, with penis erect, jumped off his partner and came toward me. I slammed the door and ran down the hall. I dashed up two flights, found 411, banged on that door, then opened it. Nobody there. Midway to the fifth floor, I stopped. He would take her to where her mother was killed. That was how he would cover it. He knew that the guidance counselor had warned Sweet Thing about Thelma Lee's obsession with her dead mother. He would make her prediction come true.

I ran down to the third-floor landing and onto the floor. Thelma's words came back, about spirits living in the place where they died, and I thought about her mother, whose legacy had caused one daughter's death and who never knew the truth.

I took off my shoes and walked barefoot to 311, careful to be quiet, and stood outside the door to get my bearings. I leaned toward the door and heard nothing. I unlocked it, thankful that this cheap motel had no security chains. I cracked it, peeked inside.

A noose dangled from the light fixture in the ceiling. I knew how he would use it. A knife was on the dirty carpet, still stained with blood. Thelma Lee lay sprawled across the bed, her mouth stuffed with her black T-shirt, her hands handcuffed behind her back. She rocked back and forth, sobbing as she did so. She saw me, and I put my finger to my lips. A light came into her eyes. The toilet flushed, and she began to tremble. I stepped back into the hall, closed the door, left it cracked. Jimson Weed grabbed Thelma Lee and shook her hard, muttering as he did so.

"I killed you once, now I got to do it again? Why you got to come back from the dead, Lily Sweets? Why you got to come back from the dead?" He swung his arm around her neck, holding her in the crook of his elbow, choking off her breath in what cops call the "sleeper hold." Soldiers knew it, too, I remembered. Trained killers like he used to be. It can kill a person in moments or render them uncon-scious. She fell against him, head limp on her chest. He tossed her on the bed, then slowly dragged the bed directly under the noose. I guessed what he would do. He would hang her from it and watch as it choked out her life.

I had to go in now. I didn't have a choice. Surprise was my only weapon.

I banged into the room like some crazed action hero, screaming at the top of my voice, swinging my arms around my head like a broken windmill. Stunned, he fell back as I heaved my body into his, throwing him off balance, knocking him to the floor. But he landed near the knife, grabbed it quick, headed toward me. I felt the blade slide across my throat, not deep enough to cut, but close enough to tell me he would kill us both without hesitation.

My thoughts came like they say they do when you're going to die, randomly with no rhyme or reason: my last words to Jamal and my first night with Basil Dupre; the sound of my brother's laughter and the morning Jamal was born; Jake's glee when he fried up oysters and, for some crazy reason, that bottle of bourbon I hadn't shared with Wyvetta Green. I closed my eyes, praying that death would come quickly and my son told gently.

"Jimson. Why you doing this, honey? Why you doing this?" It was Miss Edna Sweets, Jimson Weed's Sweet Thing, black handbag in hand, about to change it all. She stood for a moment taking things in, then ran to Thelma Lee, cradling her in her arms.

The knife left my throat; I could breathe.

"Let me do what I come for, Sweet Thing, and we can go home. It will be like it was before, like it supposed to be," he said.

She stared at him incredulously, stroking her niece's head resting in her lap.

"They mean you harm, Sweet Thing. All of them. This one, the girl, they all mean you harm." He lowered his voice and spoke in a haunted whisper. "And Lily keep coming back, baby. She won't stay dead; she keep coming back."

Sweet Thing rose from the bed, confused by his words. "What you mean, Jimson? What you talking about?" She walked toward him, ready to offer him comfort as she always had, as she thought she always would.

And I realized then what he'd said. It was the name that told me, the name Lilah refused to use. It wasn't Lilah Love but Lily Sweets who haunted him—Edna Sweets's daughter, the beginning of it all.

"You going to murder Thelma Lee like you murdered her mother,

Lily?" I said, my voice surprisingly reasonable, like I was asking him the time of day. My new "weapon of surprise" was stronger than the last one; it came down hard. He drew back, dropping his hands to his sides as dread and confusion filled his eyes. There was silence then, so deep and thick it seemed no words could cut it, then Sweet Thing began to scream, a sound both ragged and desperate. He forgot about me then and fixed his gaze on her, and when he spoke, his voice was low and heavy as if it came from another place.

"That devil Treyman Barnes brought me here, selling women like he did, and he sold me her for an hour. She was demanding more money than I had, teasing me about having nothing, laughing at me like evil women do, and it made me so mad, I slapped her, and she laughed some more, and I couldn't stop, and I did what I had to do."

I saw him as he must have looked that night, filled with rage and loathing for every living thing. Treyman Barnes's business had been drugs and women, and he had found an easy buyer in this soldier home from war who couldn't forget the killing lessons he had learned.

" 'Miss Edna Sweets,' she whispered in my ear, and I promised myself I'd take care of you because of what I done. But her Lily brought it back. Brought him back, after all these years. And after all these years, he knew me."

"You stabbed my only daughter dead like she was nothing, didn't you?" she asked him plain as day.

"She wasn't nothing but a half-white whore," he said.

And Sweet Thing reached into her handbag, took out that .22, and shot him through the heart, her aim straight and sure, as he had taught her.

NOBODY KNEW WHAT MADE Jimson Weed snap like he did. It could have been Lily Sweets come back as Lilah Love, snatching cash and giving grief. Or maybe this new war, so much like the other, unleashed demons he'd tried to forget. Or maybe he just woke up one morning and went plumb out of his mind. That could be the truth of it, too.

I do know one thing, though: truth will out in the end, and to quote Edna Sweets, life do have a way of righting itself. So I told Larry Walton what was on my mind, and Wyvetta Green who *really* put the smile on my face that Friday morning. I had a down and dirty talk with Jamal about the foolish things he'd done, and advised the Sweetses and Barneses to cherish Baby Dal and bury their sorrow. As for Basil Dupre, he called on Sunday as he promised he would, and we talked sweet and long about absolutely nothing. What will become of us? I'll let you know when I do.

And *that* is the truth!

ACKNOWLEDGMENTS

THERE ARE SO MANY PEOPLE who contribute to my mysteries that it would be impossible to thank them all on one page, but I would like to give special thanks to several who have been particularly helpful with this book. Thanks to Barbara J. Kukla for her marvelous *Swing City: Newark Nightlife,* which reminded me how great Newark was—and can become again. Thank you, John Gruesser, PhD, for your continued support and for enthusiasm about my series. My thanks to Faith Hampton Childs, my good friend and great agent, and my editor, Melody Guy, for her insightful suggestions and careful editing. And, of course, thank you, family: Richard, Thembi, Nandi—and Primo, our newest member.